THE

CENTAUR

IN MY VALLEY

A Fantasy Romance

L.V. Lane

CONTENTS

CHAPTER ONE

Hope

My business in the village is resolved more quickly than I expected. I'm a seamstress, making gowns and dresses for the ladies of the village. My skills, passed down to me by my late mother, are much in demand, and I make a tidy income from my work. This is for the best, given my husband spends more time supping beer than he does trapping for pelts. My mother told me not to wed him, warned me he was no good, and then she died of the pox. I had no one, and in a low, weak moment, I accepted his proposal.

The house we live in was my mother's, my father having passed away several years earlier. Karl's only contribution to the home is supping beer I paid for.

I pray to the Goddess daily that she might resolve this mess I made with my life. The only blessing I have received thus far is the lack of a child. It would surely be a tragedy to bring an innocent life into our loveless home. I tell myself it isn't so bad. Karl is easygoing

1

and even charming when he has a mind to be. He doesn't beat me. The worst I must suffer is his attention of a night, although that has happened less lately.

I suspect he has been indiscreet, but I turn a blind eye, thinking it better all round.

Yet I have no way out. We are wedded, and the matter is closed.

So here I am, stuck with a man I don't love but don't hate either. Mary, my best friend, says he would have to step up if I were with child. Maybe he would, or maybe this mess would be a thousand times worse. The problem is, I do want a child, desperately so. I watch the little ones playing in the village, and my heart aches for the same joy in my life.

I sigh as I round the corner by the brook and the back wall of my cottage comes into view. My home is on the outskirts of the village, backing onto the river, which, although wide, is shallow and easily crossed.

I hear voices.

Who could it be?

Is Karl already into his beer and talking to himself?

I slow. A prickling on the back of my neck alerts me to discord. Hearing two voices, I recognize the timbre of one being Karl. The other is feminine.

Confused when they appear to be emanating from my open bedroom window, I stop, my heart racing with troubling thoughts. I tell myself it is something innocent, that he wouldn't dare to be indiscreet in our marriage bed. Yet the ringing in my ears and a dizzy sensation are driving me toward conclusions I am reluctant to draw.

I told myself I wasn't bothered if he was with someone else, but the truth is that now I'm presented with the possibility, I am. I think of how he was when we first met, how charming he was, how he would bring me flowers he picked himself and tease me and make me blush, but those days soon disappeared. The reality of living with someone who has no zest for life is wearing on the soul. I don't possess complex wants or desires. A loving husband, children, enough food on the table, and a roof over my head is the summation of my dreams. That such a family might live in health, and that I might live to watch my children flourish and have children of their own, is a simple hope of mine.

Hope—that is my name, but of late, I feel unworthy of the title.

Reluctantly, I draw closer to the open window, where the shutters are open. On seeing it was a warm and pleasant day, I threw them open just this morning, only the earlier pleasantness has gone. It feels colder and filled with foreboding. I hear the giggling as I step up to the windowsill, and there I stay, not yet ready to look. I should, for it may be nothing.

"Are you sure she's not with child?" I recognize the voice of Fiona, a witchy lass from the village who is always batting her lashes at my husband like he is not a married man.

"Nay, lass, Hope is not with child. I've not bedded her in more than a moon month."

Fiona giggles. "But how could you tell? She's so fat, she might be nearly due, and you wouldn't have a clue."

Heat floods my cheeks.

Karl chuckles.

I think I'm going to be sick.

"She has her moon blood, foolish lass. The Goddess does not favor a man who abandons a pregnant wife."

My chest heaves. I wanted a way out. Is this it? If so, why do I feel so cold?

"So we really are leaving?" Fiona asks.

"Aye, lass, I said we would. I just need to find where she hides her coin bag and the few jewels from her ma. I know she has them squirreled away."

Goodness, they are planning to leave, taking my mother's jewelry!

"Have you looked under the floorboards? What about old teapots? My ma used to hide a coin purse in an old teapot on the sideboard. If I had some time in the house, I reckon I could find it."

"No, she'll be back this afternoon, and besides, you shouldn't come round here."

"I don't like the barn, as the hay makes me itch. Will there be enough for us to buy a house? Got my heart set upon a little cottage somewhere, just like this."

"More likely enough for lodgings," Karl replied. "Maybe food for a bit, then we'll need to find work."

"Work? But I thought we'd have enough to live in leisure?"

Karl suddenly groans, and Fiona chuckles. "Goddess, lass! I can't think straight when you're doing that."

"I'm not sure about this leaving business now," Fiona says. "Why do we have to leave at all? We could stay here, if she were gone."

"She's not gonna leave. It's her ma's house and has been in the family for generations."

"I know a lass in Oldham who put rat poison in her husband's tea," Fiona continues. "He was a mean bastard and used to beat her. No one would know. Then we could stay here and live off her stash of money."

My knees go weak. I brace my hand against the stone cottage wall, for fear I may collapse.

Karl laughs, a nervous kind of laugh.

A whimper escapes my tightly sealed lips.

"What was that?" Karl says.

Fiona giggles again.

I drop my basket and run.

"Hope!"

I glance over my shoulder as I reach the stream to see Karl fall out the open front door as he tries to shove his feet into his pants.

"Hope! Stop!"

4

I keep running, gathering up my skirts as I splash through the river and onto the other side.

"Hope!"

I run and run.

I take the forest path, weaving left and right, hearing Karl's heavy footsteps and crashing from behind. I cut off the trail, taking the lesser known track leading south. The sound of pursuit fades. Likely, he thinks I'm heading directly for the village.

My temper takes me all the way to the ruined farm. Here, I collapse in the shadow of an outbuilding, and falling to my knees, I heave up bile.

I feel wretched afterward, trembling from exertion, fear, and temper.

I don't love him, I tell myself. He is a lazy scoundrel who has been rutting another lass and plotting to steal my mother's heirlooms.

Yet the pain cuts all the same. The nastiness that poured from Fiona's lips as she lay in my bedroom, on my bed with my husband, was wickedness of the highest order. The village lord would have them cast out should I go to him…but they might say I was making it all up, and it would be my word against theirs. Even after all I heard, I cannot believe Karl would seek to kill me, but now I have overheard them, who knows what might happen.

They might be ransacking the home for my jewels before making off, and I will never see Karl or Fiona again.

But they might be waiting for me. They might try to kill me.

I can't believe it, yet I also can't believe what has already come to pass.

I sit back against the old wooden wall and wonder what to do.

Inside, I am numb with shock, while my mind is lost to turmoil. Is this my fault? Did the Goddess abandon me for wishing my husband away?

I don't cry, for I am too empty for that, but I am also at a loss for what to do.

I can't go back. I've never been frightened of Karl before, but for the first time, I am.

Fear, anger, and betrayal play tag with one another in my mind. I can't stay here. That much is certain.

CHAPTER TWO

Hope

Indecision holds me captive for an indeterminate amount of time. It is a warm summer day, yet a coldness has seeped under my skin and commandeered my heart. I feel alone as I sit in the shadow of a rickety old outbuilding of a long abandoned farm. Given it is summer, I could spend the night here and not catch a chill, but it is not safe to be this far from the village. Ruffians occasionally roam these lands. Perhaps they stay here.

I see no signs that people have passed through as I look around. Weeds, bushes, and even a few saplings have sprung up across the site among the cobbles that once constituted the courtyard before the formerly grand house. Two outbuildings are partially collapsed, while the main farmstead is mostly whole.

I can't stay here. I need to return to the village, yet I am still shaken. Rising, I dust off my skirt, hands shaking and perhaps also wallowing in disbelief. It is a few miles to the next village, where I have worked on occasion. Perhaps I should go there? Only I don't know anybody there well. As I stand staring out into the pretty forest, hearing the birds chirp and scenting the bloom of summer flowers in the air, it hardly seems possible that I happened upon a conversation between my husband and his lover, and that they discussed, among other things, my death.

My temper flares with indignation and outrage. How dare they? How dare she! My hands clench into fists as I walk, determined that I will return to the village. However, I will be circumspect about it. They might be waiting for me on the way in, perhaps to convince me it was a joke, but they can only watch so many paths. I still believe that they have fled, as I think that is most likely. I am well respected in the village. The lady of the house, Marigold, has commissioned many fine dresses and has always been kind to me. Then there is my dear friend, Mary, who would allow me to stay until this matter is resolved.

Only I'm not certain what anyone could do, given it is merely an overheard conversation and not a real threat. Perhaps the lord would say Karl is my husband and I must go back to him, although I cannot think of him as my husband anymore. As for Fiona, her scheming in the village is widely acknowledged, and I have heard her talking badly about other women. There is darkness in her heart and meanness in her soul. Mayhap as many people have been wronged by her as might support her.

Set upon a course, for this must be resolved, I begin walking back toward the village, but not via the way I came past my house. Who knows what nonsense Fiona might be filling my former husband's head with?

"Hope!"

The call from behind me sends a shiver down my spine.

I cannot believe Karl has followed me all the way here. Steps quickening, I throw a look over my shoulder. It is Karl, and he is on his own, wearing naught but his pants. I break into a run, not wishing to talk to him. I hear no anger in his tone, only concern. I tell myself I know this man, that he is not a murderer and only worried for me. He is no monster and might even have sent Fiona packing. Yet how do I ever trust him again? How?

I don't have an answer. My feet keep running.

"Hope!"

He is closer…gaining upon me.

"Hope. For fuck's sake, slow down. I'm not…I'm not going to hurt you. Fuck! I don't know what madness was going through Fiona's head to say such a thing. Mayhap it was only nonsense talk of a fool lass. I have been a fool too. Hope, please!"

His footsteps gain, his arms close around me, and I'm lifted from the ground. My scream rents the air.

"Steady," he says. "I won't hurt you."

He releases me instantly. My legs give out, and I collapse to the forest floor. A few paces away, Karl stands with his arms out.

The softening of his face tells me he reads my fear. "I'm sorry," he says. "I'm so sorry. We're going to leave."

Stupid tears spill down my cheeks, and my lips begin to tremble.

"I can't stay here now," he continues, arms lowering to his side. "I swear, I won't take anything."

But he was going to, I can read it in his expression. Although he is a weak man, he is not a monster.

At the sound of horses, we both turn. Blood drains from my face.

"Run," Karl says under his breath. "As fast as you can."

I do, scrambling to my feet and taking off down the path, even knowing they will be on me long before I reach the village.

Raiders, ruffians, and cutthroats. I recognize their scruffy appearance, the horses equally so, but the whoop as they charge sets the tiny hairs on my skin rising under a wave of raw terror.

We leave the path. It is harder for us but difficult for their horses to pick through the trees. Still, they are following. Their intent remains unknown. Sport perhaps? Or to rob us? Although neither of us has anything of worth, my mind turns toward those other acts a wicked man might take from a lass. I run harder and faster, but I'm already tired and I sob in frustration, knowing we cannot hope to escape.

Karl is a little ahead of me and to my left. Behind comes the heavy tread of chase, the snap and crack of branches. My breath whistles through my throat, while my thighs and lungs are on fire.

A jubilant cry accompanies an arm snaking around my waist.

I scream. My eyes shoot toward Karl. He turns back, stops, and then looks over his shoulder. More raiders are coming, three...no four. "Karl!"

I see the indecision written upon his face before he turns and runs.

"No!"

He cannot win against them should he stay. How could he? Yet the sight of him running into the forest, leaving me to the mercy of men who I have every reason to believe are merciless, is the sharpest, keenest of blows. Despair swallows me, one ragged pant and one retreating footstep at a time. With his abandonment, all hope is dashed.

The men do not pursue him. They chuckle and call out crude insults as they round on me. I fight against my captor. I cannot escape one, and there are five of them now. The man holding me laughs as he drops me to the forest floor. I scramble up and make a dash for it. Another man snatches me up and tosses me back. I rise and try to run again, but a different man captures me this time and drops me in between them. They all laugh, and I make no further attempts. They are having fun with me, playing with me in one of the callous games of evil men.

My chest rises and falls unsteadily as I assess the gaps and potential weaknesses in the loose circle they have formed.

"Go on then," one of them says, a filthy man with lank, greasy hair who is missing his front two teeth. He nudges me with his boot. I suck in a sharp breath and scramble away within the confines of their ring. "Make a run for it. We'll let you go, lass. Just having a bit of fun. Go on, off ya go."

He steps to the side, presenting an opening. When others chuckle, my eyes dart between them. Is this another game? Or are they really letting me go? I think about Karl running toward the village. Surely, he will call for help.

I convince myself that while Karl is not good, he is assuredly not bad, and he would not abandon me. Either way, the village is two miles away. I scramble to my feet and dash for the gap, breaking free of the circle.

The men all cheer, and another one snags me. They fall to laughter, well pleased with their cruel ruse.

"Let's get back to the horses," the one holding me says. "Mayhap the one that got away will round up the villagers."

I fight in earnest now because even if Karl does reach the village and calls for help, it is a fair distance away and these men have horses. My fate is sealed once they get me on a horse and ride.

I scratch and scream until a hand clamps over my mouth.

"We got ourselves a wild filly here," the man holding me says. My struggles do not trouble him. For all they are villains, they are powerful, and I am like a tiny toy within their hands.

"Maybe we should rut her?" the toothless one suggests. "Just to quiet her down. A couple of slaps and a swift rutting will make her much more manageable."

"We need to get the fuck away," another says. "Those villager types can turn mean when you try to snatch one of their womenfolk, and this one here is a pretty little morsel. They'll be after us with pitchforks in no time. No, better we ride away. That old ruin at Fordham is not too far away. We can have some fun without interruption."

I struggle harder, twist this way and that, arch my back and kick my legs. The wretchedness of my situation settles over me like a thick, cloying blanket, smothering me with a heaviness that saps the last of my energy. I pray to the Goddess for mercy, for her to forgive my weak thoughts in wishing my husband away. If I had spent more time encouraging him, been loving and forgiving, as the Goddess herself beseeches in her teachings, rather than turning him away, I might not be in this mess. I pray Karl is swift.

Yet it is all too late now as they close in on their horses. The toothless one pulls out a rag from a saddlebag and secures it around my head, muffling my squeals. My hands and ankles are bound with coarse rope before I am tossed facedown over the saddle. The ground sways, making me nauseated, as the horse shies. The man who mounts behind me plants a hand on the center of my back and urges his horse forward.

I close my eyes against a wave of dizziness as the horse surges into a canter. They ride, taking me far from my village and the only life I know.

CHAPTER THREE

Calden

A scream, feminine and ripe with terror, rends the air.

My hooves thump and skitter against the loamy forest floor as I come to a halt. I pivot, turning in the direction of the sound. "What is this nonsense about?" I mutter under my breath, my fist tightening around the handle of my spear.

There is a ruined castle not far away from here, a legacy of the era of men, when they held greater power over these lands. The centaurs took the lands back many centuries ago, reclaiming what was rightfully ours, but that sound was human, female, and not a playful scream of mischief. It was one of distress.

My hindquarters tighten then flex as I kick off and charge down the narrow forest pathway, weaving left then right. One of the younger scouts mentioned he had seen evidence of fires in the old ruin when he passed through a few weeks ago.

Raiders, ruffians, cutthroats, and villainous scum—they have many names, but they are all a scourge on society, who prey on weakness. The rest are warmongers and ever intent upon claiming what is not theirs. I have no time for such humans, and little time for any humans, save those who live within our herd, choosing the ways of the Goddess.

No civilized being enjoys the sound of a woman in distress.

I charge into the clearing, just as another scream tips ice into my veins. I take in the scene in an instant. Horses are tethered to one side of the castle ruin, while before it stands five scruffy men. Their heads swing my way. On the ground between them is a young woman, face grubby and lined with tear tracks. Her skirts are rucked up, and two of them are holding her down.

My warrior blood rises, sensing what this is about. I don't ask questions. Perhaps I should? A centaur is not blessed with patience. The men before me are not good, and it will be my pleasure to return them to the Goddess, where she might administer an eternity of suffering, as they deserve.

I strike swiftly, spear skewering the first man, before wrenching it free. He collapses to the floor, hand on his belly and the mortal wound I leave behind.

The rest scatter. No mind, I am faster. The next man takes the strike right through his neck—a clean blow. He collapses, twitching and jerking as blood spews from the fatal wound. The following two are taken down in swift succession as they make for the pathway. The last man has a head start but is easy prey before me, a centaur. My rage is powerful. I hamstring him and watch the bastard crawl. I have half a mind to string him up as a lesson to others.

Until I remember the woman lying upon the floor, so I finish him off with my spear. Stabbing through the center of his back, I slam him into the ground and twist the spear for good measure before jerking it out.

The distant sound of sobbing tears my focus from my grim task, and I turn, trotting back to the old, ruined castle.

I come to a stop on the edge of the clearing. Three bodies lie on the ground, and between them is a sobbing woman. Beyond her, I can see five horses for the five men I killed. The danger is past, but now the fallout awaits me.

Spear in hand, I approach slowly, not wanting to spook the poor maiden, lest she run into further danger. There is no scent of their seed on her, thankfully, but who knows what other torment she has suffered by their hands.

Her eyes widen as I near, and she lowers her head. "Milord! Thank you!" More words tumble out in an incoherent babble.

The woman is frightened witless. Stabbing the butt of my spear into the ground beside her, I lower to my knees. Wide, pretty brown eyes peer up at me before she flicks them away. Goddess, this broken woman is a true beauty, with her long auburn hair and those thick, tear dampened dark lashes rimming her eyes. I take her chin carefully in hand and tip her face to meet mine, finding a cute little button nose and plump pink lips. As my eyes drift lower, I note with flared nostrils that her bodice has been torn and her generous tits all but spill out. I feel an unexpected tightening in my gut. Many centaurs take human mates, for they are considered highly prized. I've had no interest, although I find the women of the village comely and they make no secret of their interest in catching my eye. I'm a warrior within our herd, but my ways and needs are particularly rough. It's true that the Goddess does change human mates to meet our needs, but I've always shied away from such couplings, thinking myself too brutish for their softness.

Still, I notice them, just as I notice the woman kneeling before me.

Her body is ripe in every way, from her generous hips to her lush tits and her full lips that are indeed Goddess-sent to wrap perfectly around a cock, yet today, and in light of her trauma, I feel the stirrings of tenderness rather than lust. "What are you doing here?"

I ask. "How did these villainous men get you?"

"I—They come across me in the forest. I was—It is a complicated story," she says in a rush, shaking like a leaf.

"There is a stream nearby. Please allow me to take you. You may drink some water and wash your hands and face. It may go a little way toward calming your nerves." It might also rid her of the touch of these villainous men.

"Thank you, milord."

Her use of a title makes me want to smile. "I am going to pick you up, lass."

"I—Oh!"

Scooping arms under her legs and around her waist, I swing her up into my arms and rise. Retrieving my spear, I carry her to the stream, where I set her down. I stand attentively a few paces away as she drinks before washing her hands and face in the water. There is a strange quietness about her as she completes this task. As she settles back on the grassy bank, I ask, "Where are you from?"

"Melwood," she says.

Only I'm not thinking about how far away Melwood is. My fingers tighten on my spear as I see a ring upon her marriage finger. "Where is your husband?" I demand, voice harsher than it might be with a young woman who has suffered such events.

She follows the line of my sight to her finger. Her lips tighten, and she surprises me when she tugs viciously on the tiny metal band.

I frown. "What are you doing?"

"It won't come off." She growls over her task, the earlier quietness all gone. I'm about to wade in on the matter, lest she hurt herself in this frenzy, when it finally comes off. She tosses it into the river in a fine display of temper that has me torn between amusement and worry.

"Well then," I say. "What was that about?"

"I overheard my husband talking to his lover," she says, tone laced with bitterness.

My chest tightens at the folly of men and their weaknesses. When a centaur commits to a mate, he commits for all his life. Marriage or mating, it is an equal and sacred bond. "What was he talking about?" I ask, although the fact he has a lover at all charges my fury.

Her lips quiver. "He was going to rob me, take my mother's jewels, and flee with his lover."

I snort a little whinny. I want to say good riddance but know little of the circumstances, nor of her feelings toward this man. She has just tossed their ring into the river, but perhaps she loves him and it was merely casting the symbol of their joining aside in a state of confusion and she will soon wish it back.

"Then—" The poor woman can barely get the words out. "Then *she* said something about putting poison in my tea."

My temper flares. What is wrong with these people?

"I ran. My husband ran after me." She sends an anxious look my way. "Karl's not a bad man." She turns away, looking toward the river. "But he's not a good man either. I do not love him. He is lazy and spends more time supping beer than working. I prayed to the Goddess to free me from the bonds. This is all my fault! I wished to be free and now I am!"

I am compelled by her story and yet still confused. "How did you come to be with raiders?"

"My husband said he was sorry, that he wouldn't take any of the things but he would leave, and that's when the raiders came."

"Your husband is dead?"

She shakes her head. "He ran for the village." My fist tightens around my spear handle. What kind of cowardly scum leaves his woman alone? "To get help. There were five raiders. He couldn't hope to defeat them."

Hope

I can't read the proud centaur well, but I sense his censure. The reasons for this wild confession become confused in my mind. I want to look favorable in his eyes, which is nonsense, given the circumstances. Tall, muscular beyond belief, and possessing a deadly grace, he scattered the criminals who took me. I still can't comprehend how swiftly he dispensed with them.

His scent is spicy, and it kicks off a fluttering low in my belly. My nipples harden to stiff peaks, and my breasts flush with arousal as his eyes pass over them. His coat is a stunning ivory color with a little gray dappling, and his hair and tail are a pure, luminous white. Unquestionably, he is handsome. But he is also a centaur, a beast, and a master of the forest, for all other creatures must surely bow before such a powerful, magnificent male.

"I have rescued you," he says, and my eyes warily meet his. "Do you understand the ways of centaurs?"

I swallow. My flutter shifts lower, pooling heat in my womb. I nod slowly. "Yes, milord, I do." There are many tales about centaurs. Some say that they snatch up lasses and take them away, bewitching them and slaking their lust upon them until they are nothing but a shell. Had I thought on the matter earlier, I might have found such stories shocking. Yet for all he is beastly, he does not strike me as a beast, nor the ravager of reluctant women.

The more I think about it, the more confident I am that such a male would not need to force his attention on anyone. More likely, they would fall at his feet and beg him.

"Then you will know it is customary to repay the debt with one moon month of your life."

"I—" I stop, not quite daring to put thoughts to words, yet I must. "What would you do with me? Would I be like…a servant?"

"You would be whatever I wish you to be," he says, eyes narrowing and tone turning harsh, reminding me that he is the master, and I, merely a lass now in his debt.

His hooves stamp against the soft riverbank, and my eyes lower to the juncture of his strong hindquarters. Goddess, the very tip of his cock is huge and black and emerging a small way from the lighter hair-covered sheath.

"Do you accept your debt?" he asks, dragging my attention from that arresting sight.

I blush to the roots of my hair. Goddess! He just caught me staring at his cock! I must swallow several times before I can get the words past my lips. "Milord, I do."

"My name is Calden. No title is required." He smiles, transforming his handsome face to breathtaking.

"And I am Hope, mi—Calden." His name has a pleasing ring to it. Saying it lends an intimacy to the moment.

"A pretty name," he says. "Can you ride, Hope?"

"Ride?" I squeak out, ashamed by the wayward direction of my thoughts.

"The thugs who took you left several horses, and I believe they will not need them again. We have much distance to cover, and it will go swifter if you are able to ride."

"I can, milord...Calden." I wince.

Calden chuckles. "Come, lass, let us find you a suitable steed. The rest, we will take with us. I dare say they will find more compassionate owners within our herd."

I wonder what use a centaur might have with a horse, but then I remember how humans live with them, men, women, and children born of their couplings. As I rise to shaky feet, I also remind myself that a centaur is a powerful, sentient being and nothing like a horse, save they have a similar-looking part to their bodies.

I hold my torn bodice in place as Calden trots back to the clearing before the ruin.

I follow, coming to a stop when I see the bodies. After they took me, they traveled all day long, stopping only briefly to water the horses. Then, on reaching this ruinous ancient castle, they turned their depraved focus to me, eager to explore their prize. Fear, cold and cloying, grips me as I relive the past terror.

"Wait there, Hope," Calden says, seeing me falter. "I will bring a horse to you."

Only I cannot unsee what is before me—the remains of the cruel men who were intent upon raping me, who wanted to use me for their pleasure, uncaring of how it might have hurt me. My closeness to such a terrible fate brings a full body tremble.

Thrusting his long spear into the ground butt first, Calden trots to me.

Goddess, his size is so intimidating. It is all I can do not to flee. I do turn, panicked, a tiny gasp escaping me when he lifts me up.

"Steady. You have had a fright. I will not harm you, I swear it, but I cannot allow you to run blindly into the forest. Night is approaching. Evil can take many forms and I hate to caution you, but worse than these raiders are present after dark. I dare say you have heard things about centaurs, about us snatching lasses away and sating our lusts upon them. I assure you that it is nonsense, just tall tales spread to instill fear where none is needed."

Only it is not fear I am feeling anymore, not now I am in his arms. The part of him I touch feels entirely human, this mighty warrior with a shock of pure white hair. His eyes are hazel and kind. They also hold heat. My belly clenches, and unmistakable dampness gathers between my thighs.

"I am fine now, milord," I squeak out.

His nostrils flare, and he snorts in a way that reminds me of a horse. Goddess, does he scent me?

The spell is broken when he turns on the spot and carries me over to a horse. Settling me in the saddle, he passes me the reins. The horses, I note, all flick their ears back and forth before turning attentively toward Calden.

"We must ride fast," he says. "The other horses will follow. If you find yourself tiring, call out."

I nod.

CHAPTER FOUR

Calden

I about-face and set off at a trot. The horses are shy of a centaur, sensing our predatory nature, but they follow, with Hope's horse behind mine like the good herd beasts they are.

I don't want her on a fucking horse. I want her with me, yet I do not trust this riot taking place inside my body. My cock threatens to surge from the sheath, allured by her scent, which is sweet, despite the filth of travel.

This is not me. I am not the kind of male who is weakened by mere scent. Not only her scent, but her presence stirs me in ways I have never been before. I tell myself I'm only taking her away from danger and a bastard husband. I fully expect him to have fled, as she indicated they would. I could take her home. If the scum was still around with his lover, it would be my pleasure to administer justice and see him tossed from her village. Still, the ways of humans are strange to me. A woman whose husband has run away could be shunned or blamed for all I know.

I want to protect her.

I want to do a lot more than that, but the need to have her in my home, where I can keep her safe to my satisfaction, is an imperative that cannot be ignored.

Although I set off at a trot, I soon determine that she is competent on a horse and pick up my pace.

Yet even this does not please me. I question my actions. Why would I put her on a horse when I want her with me? Only a quagmire of emotions assaults me. A moon month I have claimed, and now I must deal with this bargain of my making. I could have taken her back to her village, yet the mere thought of parting brings a shake to my hands, so there is no hope for it.

The rest of the horses follow as is their nature. Better for all of us to be back at the herd before night falls, given there are beasts in this forest that can make hardened raiders quake with fear. As we break through the cover of the trees, the lake surrounding my village comes into view, glistening in the late evening sun.

I sense as much as hear her sob of distress from behind. I find Hope hanging down, one arm clinging to the horse's neck. I curse under my breath, calling myself every kind of monster for allowing her to suffer because I can't get my libido under control, and gather her up into my arms, the horror that she might have fallen giving way to tenderness.

"I'm sorry, milord," she says.

"Calden," I correct. Now that she is in my arms, it feels right. "There, foolish woman, you should have spoken up. You will stay here until we reach home." My spear is awkward, but I will make fucking do. I trot on, and the horses, unsettled with the turn toward dusk, follow meekly behind.

"Hail, Calden!" the two centaurs on duty call.

"Hail!" I reply.

"What have you got there?" asks the left-hand centaur, Gael. He nods his head toward the woman in my arms, grinning broadly.

"You can see what I have." My scowl only draws his chuckle. Gael claimed a human mate only last year. Our herd leader, Axton, similarly claimed a mate. It would seem we are all succumbing to the same allure.

"I'd never have thought it with you," Gael teases.

"She is tired and has suffered much trauma," I say bluntly. "Send for Celeste."

"Aye," Gael says, his face instantly softening as he eyes the curvy young woman who has buried her nose against my chest. "I'll go at once. Are you going back to your home?"

I nod, realizing that there is no other place I might take her that is acceptable to me.

Gael pivots and trots off without further questions. He understands, as I do, the Goddess' hand at work in placing such a beauty in my path.

As I trot for my home, the horses following, I spot Peter, a young centaur lad. When I hail him, he trots over, grinning. "Can you stable these new horses, lad?"

"Gladly, Calden," he calls. "I'll take good care of them."

My home is a sturdy round structure close to the center of the village. As we draw up to the entrance, Hope lifts her head.

"This is my home, Hope," I say. "You will stay here for your moon month debt." She is exhausted, and the events are catching up with her. "Celeste is a healer here and will be along presently."

"I am fine," she says. "A little tired, that is all." She rouses a little as I sit her on the table, peering over the side. "Goodness! The table is very high."

I smile, brushing her long auburn hair over her shoulder, resisting the urge to cup her pretty flushed cheeks. I will not rush this, especially given what she has been through, but instead, let nature run its course. As is the way within our herd, nothing shall happen that she does not also desire.

Yet I'm hopeful, and her reaction to my scent is unmistakable. Already, I sense her body is changing. Slick pools between her thighs, if the way she squeezes them together is any indication. My eyes lower, taking in her plump tits and the ample swell of her hips. My mouth waters for the taste of her, and my cock pushes out from its sheath, feeling hot and heavy with need. I berate myself. Hope has been inside my home for moments and is further traumatized.

My cock has a mind of its own.

She shudders as if reading the wayward direction of my thoughts, and her pretty tits quiver, threatening to spill out of her gown.

I want her naked. Most centaurs do not concern themselves with clothing. Even the humans among us tend to wear less, if they dress at all, certainly far less than this hideous, heavy gown. Tomorrow, I will find her something more suitable to wear.

A knock sounds on the door, and Celeste, our herd healer, enters. "Hail, Calden," she says, smiling kindly at Hope as she walks over to join us.

"I found her at the mercy of raiders," I say.

Settling her satchel on the table, Celeste turns to me. "If we might have a moment, Calden," she says.

Although I cannot bear to be a room's length away from Hope, I go. I light a couple of lanterns and hang them from the hooks in the ceiling, then make a show of lighting the stocked fire and putting some water on to boil, staying away from the two women, who talk quietly. I send the odd glance their way to satisfy myself that all is still well.

As the water comes to a boil, Celeste calls out, "If we might have the hot water for the tea now, Calden?"

I carry the water over and fill the pot she has readied, likely with something to help Hope to sleep.

I share a look with Celeste after she hands the cup to Hope. Her

L.V. LANE

small, encouraging smile tells me there is nothing worse than what has obviously happened to the young woman now within my care. "Hope is heart sore but hail," Celeste says. "Nothing that a little time and rest won't heal."

Relief and tenderness crash over me. I will need to go slower than might be usual when a centaur and maiden cross paths, but I trust in the Goddess to guide this. Not all women take to a life among the centaurs. Some choose to leave. Such matters of the heart and body cannot be forced.

The two women continue to talk, so I go busy myself on the other side of the room. They talk about Hope's village, what she used to do, and all manner of nonsense, which I'm sure is intended to put her at ease.

"I'm a seamstress," Hope says, and in that unguarded moment, pride shines on her face. "I'm happiest with a needle and thread. I've been lucky to take on my late mother's clients in Melwood and the neighboring towns. Gowns and dresses were my main work, although I can turn my hand to most things."

"Centaurs do not wear so many clothes," Celeste says kindly.

"You do not?" Hope asks.

Celeste indicates her own attire, which is little more than a leather harness to cover her breasts. The beast part of her body has no need for clothes. Not all centaur females even choose this much. It is more a choice based on personal comfort.

Only now, my mind goes to thoughts of Hope's lush tits unadorned. I swallow thickly. My fucking cock has no chance of going down.

"But you have humans here?" Hope asks, looking between the two of us.

"We do," I say, trying to get the image of a naked Hope from my mind. I can only guess what lies underneath her hideous clothing, but my imagination is running rampant. "But they wear considerably less than might be expected in the human lands."

"Oh," she says softly, cheeks turning pink. "How much less?"

"I'll take my leave," Celeste says. "I'll stop by tomorrow and check that you are well."

We both thank Celeste as she leaves, closing the door on us.

"How much less?" she asks again.

"Considerably less."

Head lowering, she goes back to sipping her tea, no longer meeting my eyes.

"How are you feeling?" I ask. "Would you like something to eat?"

"Very tired," she says before breaking into a huge yawn. "But not hungry. I just want to sleep…if there is perhaps a blanket I might have."

I take the empty cup from her hands. "I will take you to my bed."

She glances about. "Your bed?"

"Yes, Hope, my bed." There is only one bedroom in a centaur's home, save for when they take a mate and add rooms for the arrival of their young. I realize I will need to have my stable prepared for a human. My bedroom holds only the pallet bed. Although there is room for the saddle, I never bothered having one, as I never desired to bed a woman.

A thick tendril of arousal wraps around my cock at the thought of doing so now. I feel it push fully from my sheath and bite back a groan as my balls tighten, ejecting a small jet of pre-cum. I shut my mind from the image of Hope's beautiful, lush body draped over a saddle, plump breasts hanging down, thick thighs spread and strapped into place, leaving her pussy on display.

"We will sleep together," I say, adding a little determination to my tone. I will give Hope as much time as she needs, but I must have her close. "That way, I may be sure you are safe, but first, let us remove some of these heavy clothes so you may rest in comfort."

I want to strip her of all the constricting things, but I will settle for removing the heavy outer layers.

She blushes. "I don't think it would be proper," she says.

My nostrils flare. "Hope." My voice is sterner than it should be, but I cannot help myself. "You are mine for one more month. I wish you to be comfortable while we sleep. This is not open to discussion."

Her face takes on a healthy glow in the lamplight, and the scent of her arousal perfumes the air. Knees pressed tightly together, she swallows. "Yes, milord."

I raise a brow.

"Yes, Calden."

"Good girl," I say decisively, reaching for the ties that hold her torn bodice in place. "Let us remove this dreadful burden."

Seeing her beautiful tits straining the fabric, I swallow thickly, and another heady rush of pre-cum ejects from my cock. She clamps a hand to her chest as the chords come free. The lighter material of her chemise clings lovingly to her flesh.

The skirts come next, the button coming free with a pop. I will have one of the lads toss it away before she rises in the morning.

"I'm going to lift you up," I say.

"Yes, milord," she squeaks out. Then she is in my arms, and the heavy layers of her dress are stripped away. Her beautiful, lush tits mash up against my chest while my arm is full of her bottom, separated from her skin by a fine piece of material. She looks anywhere but at me, even though she's facing me, and we are intimately pressed together. I brush the hair back from her face and tip her chin up. As her eyes flash to mine, her pupils dilate.

"Are you ready for bed, love?" The endearment slips from my lips, but I won't take it back. "I'll get you some water to wash up first, hmm? The water is boiled, and it will only take a moment."

"Thank you."

I carry her into the bedroom, where a huge, layered pallet filled with furs, pelts, and soft woolen blankets woven by the village womenfolk waits for us.

"Oh, this is nice," she says. "It's so soft and smells wonderful." She blushes prettily. I'm sure she would blush twice as deeply should I tell her that it scents of my alpha musk.

I busy myself pouring a bowl of water for her, along with a cloth and soap, then I take myself outside and away from temptation. I trot straight into the lake, washing the dust, sweat, and blood from my body in the cool water. It also goes some way toward cooling my ardor.

By the time I have dried off and returned, I find Hope curled up on the bed, asleep. My chest softens with a foreign emotion. I take the dirty water and cloth away, and steeling myself, return to the bed. She has curled up on one side like she is afraid to take any space. I settle in beside her as carefully as I can before drawing her smaller body against mine. Finding her chilled, I pull a thick woolen blanket over her. "Rest, Hope. You are tired. Tomorrow, we'll find something you might do while you're here."

"Thank you, milord," she mumbles. "For everything."

The tender place in the center of my chest demands attention as her lashes lower and she drifts back into sleep. I do not understand these feelings that assault me and can only look at her in wonder. Hope is a precious gift, but there is a long road ahead of us, for she has been scarred by first a weak husband and then by weak raiders who sought to take her against her will.

Time will offer healing and perspective, but I only have one month. Afterward, if she does not accept me, I must let her go.

CHAPTER FIVE

Hope

Iwake up to the sounds of movement in the living area. I rise groggily, disorientated until everything comes crashing back. Karl, the raiders, Calden...

A thick pelt covers me. I have rested better than I have in many years, despite all the troubles. I stretch lazily and smile. Perhaps it will not be so bad spending a moon month here.

I'm curious about my new home, although a little intimidated by the centaur male, whose hooves I can hear thudding against the compacted earth floor of the hut. I feel unsettled and a little woozy. Perhaps this is an aftereffect of the tea?

No.

Turning my head to the side, I snuffle into the pelt underneath my cheek. Goodness, his scent is wonderful. Just breathing makes my tummy turn fluttery. I lie there for a while, thinking about getting up and yet not wanting to break the spell. My clothes are in the main room somewhere, yet I feel strangely decadent. This is the softest bed I've ever lain upon, making my thick, feather mattress back at Melwood seem hard and unpleasant by comparison.

As I run my fingers over the soft pelts, my nipples peak. Goodness, I am aroused, unmistakable dampness pooling between my thighs. Each tiny movement brushes the pelt against my skin, making my nipples pebble harder. When was the last time I felt this way? A very long time, perhaps never.

"I know you are awake," a stern voice says from the open doorway.

My head lifts up, and I peak over the top of the pelts to find Calden standing there, staring at me. "You are not a dream then," I say saucily.

He smiles, making his handsome face impossibly more so. His long white hair falls over his shoulders and around his clean-shaven face, while his hazel eyes dance with mirth. "I am no dream, woman. We centaurs are very real."

I smile. It is nice to smile. "May I have my dress please?"

His smile drops, and his eyes narrow.

Goodness, how rude of me to demand he fetch my dress! Given I am in his debt, it is twice as rude. "A-Apologies, milord," I stammer. "I shall collect it." I push aside the soft fur pelt and rise a little unsteadily to my feet.

"There is no dress," he says. "Did we not cover this yesterday?" He steps up to me, making me back up until I almost fall onto the bed. Then his hands clamp around my waist, and he picks me up as though I weigh nothing and carries me to the table, where he sits me down.

My face heats with a blush, and I look down. Only now do I acknowledge my state of dress, how thin the material of my chemise is, how my nipples are hardened, and the way my large breasts nearly spill out as I heave in a ragged breath.

"Steady, Hope," he says, brushing my hair back from my hot

cheek. "Centaurs do not wear clothes like that. Some of us wear no clothes at all."

I glance at him, but he does not appear angry anymore. "I shouldn't feel comfortable without my dress, milord," I say.

"Calden," he reminds me.

"Calden, please tell me where it is, so I may get it."

"The dress is gone." Stepping back, he turns and heads over to the fire, where a pot has been placed to heat.

I clamp my hands over the side of the table, not liking how high this is from the ground, nor how I am effectively trapped here while he goes about his chores. My eyes follow him, and I become distracted from my worries as I watch the play of muscles as he moves. I admit to being fascinated by the two different parts of his body. While he stood close at the table, I could almost forget that he has a beastly part. But now, as he stokes the fire, I can think of nothing else. His coat is a beautiful, dappled gray, while his pure white tail matches his hair.

Now I consider him collectively, how the two parts make one distinct creature. He is resplendent and so powerful. I cast my mind back to yesterday and how he took down the raiders, swiftly and precisely. He is the most formidable warrior I've ever seen, yet he is gentle with me. As he turns, my gaze lowers, and oh my! His cock has emerged from the sheath. The flared tip is pure black, but a short way up, it turns pink. A long thread begins to leak from the tip and stretches all the way to the floor…before it drops. I swallow.

My stomach rumbles, and he finishes turning to catch me in my perusal. Blushing, I lower my eyes. Is he aroused? Perhaps that is natural for a centaur. I wouldn't know. Those tales I heard about centaurs carrying off lasses and doing wicked things to them return to plague me. Suddenly, I am certain that he is a highly sexual creature with great needs and unnatural appetites for carnality that far exceed humans.

He trots back to me, and I look everywhere but him. The fabric across my breasts draws tighter with every breath. They seem to swell, my nipples grow ever harder, and between my thighs is the unmistakable trickling of my arousal.

What is wrong with me?

When I dare to glance, I find he stares with open interest at my quivering breasts.

"This is natural between a centaur and a woman," he says. "Do not mind it. Centaur musk is potent for some humans, but as I say, do not trouble yourself. Would you like me to take you so that you might wash?"

"I could walk, milord."

"Calden," he reminds.

"I can walk, Calden."

"But still," he says. "I should prefer to take you. The river joins the lake not far from this house. It is a good place and offers privacy."

He picks me up before I can venture to answer, and I squeak.

"Steady, Hope. No harm shall come to you."

"But I-I…" I splutter. "I can walk, Calden." I am a breath away from calling him milord again, hoping it might place a shield between us. I am pressed against his naked human part, feeling firm muscles relax and flex as he moves and bewitched by his rich scent. My hands pet the warm flesh surreptitiously as he gathers soap and a cloth and carries me out the door.

We are right in the middle of the village, where humans and centaurs hasten about their business. "Hail, Calden!" somebody calls.

"Hail!" Calden calls back.

No one gives our passage more than a cheery wave or glance as Calden carries me a short distance along a path that leads from the back of his house down to a river. Here, he stops and sets me down.

"The water is cool but pleasant," he says, handing me the soap and cloth. "I'll bring you fresh clothes."

What does he mean by fresh clothes? He has already admitted that centaurs rarely wear any, and the few humans we just passed wore naught but brief and indecent clothing made out of hide!

"Thank you. But if I had my dress, I'm sure I could..." I trail off under his narrowed eyes. "I could scrub it myself!"

His lips thin. "I'll take your chemise." He holds out his hand. "You cannot go about in the village in that."

"Oh," I say when his hand remains held out expectantly. "You wish me to take off my chemise now, while you are still here?"

"I do," he says. "Come along, woman. We do not have all day to be about this. Hand it over and then you may wash. No one else will see you here. I will be back presently."

No one else is the phrase that sticks. He shall surely see me.

My body has curves, a full figure. When I think about Fiona's cruel words, my confidence wanes. Calden will be used to beautiful, strong centaur females like Celeste and be repulsed by me.

"I'm still waiting," he says, only now he is staring at my breasts. He is not even pretending to look elsewhere. I do not hate my body, for it is the one the Goddess gave me, but I also understand my imperfections. I try telling myself that it doesn't matter whether Calden finds me desirable or not. Yet the way he studies me, hardly breathing, unsettles me.

As if under a spell, I gather the hem and slowly draw it up. His nostrils flare as I reach my hips, his darkening gaze now fixed on what I expose. Cheeks flushed, I draw the thin material over my head.

Naked, I no longer have the opportunity to hide as his eyes roam over me.

"Beautiful," he murmurs, and I must swallow down the lump in my throat. "I have never seen a more perfect vision of femininity."

I feel a strange catch in my chest, sensing the truth of his words, how he sees me like this. "I am a little plump," I say, like I am trying to dislodge this strange need for his approval.

He smiles, crinkling the skin in the corners of his eyes. "You are," he agrees. "Plump and pretty, as a woman should be." He motions for me to hand over the chemise. "I'll be back soon with something more appropriate for you to wear during your moon month."

I hand over the garment, and he takes it with a nod and turns. It is only now that I see what I thought was his cock is but a small part of it. Goosebumps spring up across my skin. His cock now hangs long, thick, and heavy, pre-cum leaking from the tip. His tail flicks as he trots away, revealing his potent balls nestled at the base of his cock.

If I am feminine in his eyes, then he represents the height of masculinity to me, and my body cannot help but respond. He said that my reaction was natural, that his musk influences some lasses. My thighs squeeze together as I try to ease the growing ache deep inside my core. I am wet with arousal. How will I ever get through a moon month?

CHAPTER SIX

Calden

At the risk of doing something I might live to regret, I leave her at the river. Her gorgeous body is everything I anticipated and a thousand times more. My cock hangs long and heavy, but there is no hope for it. I am a centaur. As the lore foretells, I came across a woman in my path, and she is mine now. At least that is how I wish it to be. Still, as is the way of our people, I must allow Hope the choice.

My mind drifts to thinking about how she will look when she is properly saddled, placed into position and tied down for my pleasure, as a good little human should be.

I toss her chemise into a nearby firepit, and in an attempt to cool my ardor, I make a detour toward the lake. Here, I plow straight into the cold water. By the time I finish dowsing myself, my cock is once more fully sheathed and decent, and I head for the cottage belonging to Gael and Lila.

Lila is a pretty raven-haired human, and I find her busy hanging tanned hides out to dry. She has skills in the art of tanning and picks the best pelts and furs that she prepares for clothing and bedding. While we have several tanners in the community, the human women who wear hide swear her goods are the softest. "Hail, Calden," she calls, smiling brightly.

Every centaur may take a different approach to his mate and how they might dress. Axton, our herd leader, keeps his mate naked save for a cloak, which he allows her to don when she goes outside, along with a pair of boots to keep her feet safe. Lila, by comparison, wears a hide wrap dress, and I think something similar might be appropriate for my charge. Only where Lila is slim, Hope has generous hips and tits. I've already decided her chemise, and anything of a similar nature, will not be worn by her again. She is a seamstress, and I believe she could make herself clothing given a little time, but first, I must set the tone and what is allowed.

"Is your mate home, Lila?"

"No, milord," she says. "Gael left for his patrol." Her smile turns sly. "I heard you had a moon month lass?"

"Aye Lila, I do, but she went through some trauma, being captured by raiders, when I came upon her during my deep patrol yesterday. I'd like to bring her to you later, so she can meet the women within the herd. I hope it will go some way to settling her into this life. Beside the raiders, there are other troubles she has endured, about which I hope she shall talk to you."

"I should be delighted to meet her," Lila says, face softening. "There is no easy way for a woman to come to be with a centaur, but we all trust in the Goddess when she places us in the path of our true mates. I remember well how strange and confusing a time it was. Gael did not allow me out of his sight for that moon month! I'm so excited, for you and for her. Gael often talks of how it is time you settled down."

I chuckle. "I am not there yet, but I will do everything in my power to ensure when the moon month finishes, she does not wish to leave. Now, though, I need some clothing for her."

She smirks. "You centaurs have a strange aversion to human clothes."

I shrug. A centaur wants what he wants, and we have no shame in this.

"Fine then," she says. "Tell me about your lass, and I will check what clothing can be found in the stores."

"She is close to you in height, but" —I make the sign of her curves— "fuller. Do you have aught in the stores that might work? I'm thinking of a wrap dress such as you wear."

"Aye," she says, grinning. "I will go and check. They may just show a little more skin on a fuller figure."

I'm not displeased with this… I believe Lila reads this on my face, for she throws her hands up, chuckling before disappearing into the cottage. She returns shortly later, holding a pretty, blue dyed hide wrap dress. I can't help but reflect on how it will fall lovingly around Hope's curves.

"I shall find some soft hide and supplies for when she visits, so she can make her own if she chooses," Lila says.

I take the offered dress. "My thanks, Lila. Please let me know what I can give you as recompense."

"Nothing, milord," she says. "I only ask that you bring your moon lass over when it pleases you, that I might befriend her."

"I shall, Lila," I say, already knowing the two women shall get along. I know little about Hope, but everything I've learned so far tells me she is sweet natured and holds not a bit of spite. I want her to feel welcomed here, not only by me but also by the womenfolk and the other herd members.

When I return to the water, I must steel myself, for she has finished her morning ablutions and is covered in naught but a small cloth that doesn't come close to hiding her beautiful body. She blushes prettily when she sees me arrive.

"Hail, Hope," I say. "I have brought you a dress."

Her tentative smile shifts to a frown upon seeing the dress I hold out. She looks from me to dress, to me again, face turning a bright shade of red. "Milord, where is the rest of it?"

"Calden," I correct her, feeling a familiarity in the exchange, one that wraps a layer of intimacy around us.

"But, Calden, where is the rest of it?"

"That is all there is," I say, handing it over. "This is how women who live among centaurs are clothed. It should look very strange were you to wear aught else."

She shakes her head. "I should like my chemise back please, milord." A little frost enters her tone. "And my dress."

I bite back a smile at how she seeks to put distance between us by using a title instead of my name. I sense a temper tantrum might be about to unfold. "Not possible, Hope. They are disposed of."

"Well, un-dispose of them," she says heatedly.

My eyes narrow. "You have forgotten yourself, Hope. You are in my debt for a month. You will wear this dress because I decide it. You may wear this dress, or you may choose to wear nothing. Either is acceptable to me."

"Naked?" Her blush has spread to the upper swell of her plump tits, poorly covered by the cloth. I am determined that I shall be hiding the larger clothes so that tomorrow, she will not even have that to hide behind.

"Naked," I confirm with an incline of my head.

She opens her mouth and closes it again before huffing out a little breath. "This is scandalous!" Turning her back on me, she drops the cloth.

I must bite my lower lips to stifle my groan, unable to help my thoughts from venturing toward images of her saddled, ready to be disciplined or mounted. I am sorely disappointed she does not push the matter more so I might have an opportunity to put my hands upon her bottom for a firm discipline. Gods, I need to think of something else. My cock, which had finally softened after the trip in the lake, is hard, hot, and showering pre-cum all over the forest floor.

The dress covers her ass, barely. I'm sure to catch plenty of glimpses of her beautiful body.

"Goddess!" she mutters, tugging it over her ass. "Oh! This is indecent!"

"It is not indecent," I say. "Merely indecent compared to foolish human notions of sensibility. I cannot believe the heavy dress you wore is close to being comfortable. Our bodies are meant to be free, not covered all the time. Is it not warm enough here for you to dress thusly?"

"It is warm," she agrees. Her hands are shaking with a little temper.

My palm itches. I suspect Hope will need some correction before she behaves. It will be my pleasure to administer loving discipline when necessary.

"There is not enough material!"

"Hope," I say, waiting until she glances over her shoulder at me. "I can hear a lot of complaining. Do you need some discipline before you can be good and wear what I have chosen for you?"

"I-I," she splutters. "What does that mean?"

"It means if I get any more complaining or huffing of breath, the palm of my hand will be applied to your bottom until you learn some respect."

Her eyes widen, and the heady scent of her arousal perfumes the air.

Discipline is a natural part of bonding between a centaur and his mate, which I desire Hope to become. Although given the trauma she has been through, I doubt I would use a strap, as most centaurs do, but instead only my hand. My cock spits a heavy gush of pre-cum to the forest floor, preferring the more intimate correction delivered via my hand. "You are indebted to me," I say. "You agreed to this, did you not? That means you shall obey me in all ways for the moon month. If you do not, I have no choice but to discipline you."

"Goddess," she mutters.

Her back is still to me, but I see her move her hand to her lower belly and press. My nostrils flare. "Is there a problem?"

"No, milord," she squeaks out. "No problem, at all."

"Turn around then," I say. "Let me see."

Heaving a breath, she slowly turns to face me. Her eyes are downcast. It's all I can do not to charge at her like a savage, hold her down, and rut her on the riverbank. Mounting a woman is not so easy without the aid of a saddle, which is not advised for the first time, but I am confident I could make it fucking work.

"Stunning," I say thickly. The wrap fits Hope's waist snugly but barely contains her full tits, while her ample ass and hips mean the skirt skims her pussy. It doesn't hide the tops of her thighs that now glisten with arousal, nor the way her stiff nipples are clearly visible through the material.

She nibbles on her lower lip and glances shyly at me. "You don't think it's unseemly?"

"I think it is perfect, and you, the prettiest woman I have ever seen."

I see the uncertainty on her face and call her former husband twice a fool for not knowing the beauty he had. It will be my duty and pleasure to right this wrong, to be sure she has no doubts that I find her comely, and when the time is right, to show her how she captivates me. "Come," I say. "I will take you to meet the women in the village. We have two human mates who joined us not long ago. Chastity and Lila are often together of a day, although Chastity is plump with child now and might not be about so early. Would you like that?"

"Yes," she says, smiling tentatively. "Oh!"

I pick her up, enjoying how her naked bottom rests against my arm.

CHAPTER SEVEN

Hope

He carries me through the village like I am incapable of walking. Nobody pays us any mind, although it is busier than when he took me to the river and more people call out greetings. I've never felt so uncomfortable in my life.

Soon, we arrive at a small cottage, which is round in design like Calden's, where a young lass is tending to some work in her garden. As we draw near, I see that she is working some colored hide into clothing. The pretty blue of the one in her hands matches my dress. She stands, and I see she wears a wrap dress similar to mine…except that she is smaller than me in both the hip and breast, so she appears decent when compared to me. Her smile is bright and welcoming. Her raven hair shimmers in the sunlight and falls all the way to her waist.

"Hail, Calden," she calls out as I am placed to the ground, where I hastily seek to straighten out my dress. Her dress, I amend.

"Hope, this is Lila, the mate of Gael."

"Pleased to meet you," I say.

Lila surprises me by giving me a hug. It is strange, if a little forward, but it also feels nice, so I hug her back.

"Come," she says. "Why don't we have some tea?"

I glance back toward Calden. I assuredly did not anticipate my moon debt would involve having a cup of tea.

"I'll return later, Hope," Calden says before turning and trotting away. My eyes follow him, this proud, noble beast who makes me a little breathless.

A gentle nudge on my shoulder stirs me from my perusal to find Lila wearing a knowing look.

"He is a fine warrior," she says. "You are not the first lass to look longingly after him, but you are the first he has accepted into his home."

"I-I was…" I want to argue with her observation that I was mooning after him, but clearly, I was.

She laughs. "Come on. I'll put some tea on, and then we'll go and sit on the bench in the shade of the oak tree."

I follow her inside, finding a layout similar to Calden's, except there is a single high chair at the tall farmhouse table.

"You have a chair," I say before I can consider how rude that might sound.

"I do, although it took some time before Gael bought one. When a centaur takes a human mate, he has one commissioned, along with other things that he might need." Lila busies herself, putting the kettle on to boil. After gathering a pot and cups from a shelf, she sets them out on a tray.

"Can I help?" I ask.

"Thank you, Hope. There are some cookies in that big blue jar on the shelf. Let's put a few on the tray to take out." She passes me a wooden bowl. "Best put plenty on. Chastity will be joining us, and she loves cookies."

I busy myself with the task as she pours water over the tea in the pot.

"We shall sit in the sun under the oak tree. How does that sound?"

"Wonderful," I say, and really, it does sound wonderful. "So centaurs need to commission furniture when they take a mate?" I ask, curious about this.

"Of course, though only if they mate a human, otherwise they would have no need for them and they would just get in the way. While there are humans in the village, they are few in number."

I nod slowly. "That makes sense." To the left of the hearth is what I presume to be their bedchamber, with the curtain drawn across. I think about the soft bed in Calden's home and how pleasant it was to nestle in his arms last night. A shiver runs through me as I remember how it felt to have his scent surrounding me, how his otherworldly power made me feel safe. It seems so silly, for I have known Calden for a day, yet I feel more toward him than I ever did toward my husband. Thankfully, Lila is busy with the tea and does not notice.

"All ready," Lila says brightly. We head out the front and around the side, past a small garden full of vegetables with runner beans, cabbages, lettuces, carrots, and a few other things. Beyond, where the garden meets the forest, is a broad oak tree with a long, human bench underneath and a small tree stump crafted into a table of sorts.

She sets the tray down, just as a call comes from the front of the house.

"Chastity," Lila says, beaming. "I hoped you might be along. This is Hope. She is in Calden's moon debt."

"I'm so excited!" Chastity says like this is the best news she has heard, making me even more confused about this whole moon debt.

Chastity, I note as she draws near, is wearing a long cloak that cannot hope to disguise a belly in the late stage of pregnancy. She is blonde, tiny, and pretty. "Welcome, Hope!" She smiles as she eyes the cookies on the tray. "Cookies. Your oat cookies are my favorite."

Lila laughs. "Now you are teasing me. I know your mate feeds you well."

Chastity blushes as she joins us on the bench. Why would she blush?

Lila pours the tea and passes around the cookies.

"Chastity is mated to our herd leader, Axton," Lila explains. It becomes apparent quickly that the two women are firm friends, and an easy conversation flows around us. They ask me about my home, what I did, and all the things that led me into Calden's path. I share some parts, and I skim over the others that are still too raw.

"My late husband died of the pox," Chastity says. "I picked herbs to make a living and kept chickens for eggs, but it was hard. I had ventured far from home and was injured when Axton found me."

"I was cornered by wolves," Lila says.

"I found my husband with his lover, and I ran from home," I say. I don't go into the details of him abandoning me to the raiders, nor that his lover, Fiona, wanted him to poison me. "That was when the raiders found me."

"I'm sorry to hear your husband treated you thus," Chastity says. "And goodness, that must have been terrifying. They did not harm you, did they, before Calden found you?"

I shake my head. "No," I say, although the memories of being held down by them, cruel fingers pulling up my dress, is fresh.

"That is a small mercy," Lila says. "But perhaps all things happen for a reason. Do you trust in the Goddess?"

"I think I do, only there are some days when I wonder if she has other, more pressing matters to tend to."

"There," Lila says, taking my hand and gently squeezing. "I do believe she watches all and is powerful enough that she can oversee everyone at once. She doesn't always intervene swiftly, but perhaps that's because she must plan when the matter is complicated. You are here, and surely that is part of her design."

Only I don't know what *here* means. "I'm only here for a month," I say, frowning. "I am indebted to Calden, which is a little confusing. I expected I might be a servant...not drinking tea."

They both giggle.

"Well," Chastity says in the manner of one smoothing over a matter. "Tell us what you think of Calden? I know you have only known him for a small amount of time, but he is a proud warrior, and many female centaurs have sought to catch his eye."

"They have?" I ask before I can think better. They would be beautiful together, strong yet sensual. My heart pounds a little quicker, imagining him with such a mate. He is a virile male...as evidenced by how swiftly he dispensed with the raiders who sought to defile me. "He is handsome," I admit. "And a formidable warrior."

They both nod knowingly. "No harm shall come to you under Calden's watch," Lila says. "Save a little embarrassment with their choice of clothing."

"I'm not allowed to wear anything underneath this cloak," Chastity confesses. "The moment I enter the home, I must take it off."

"You're naked in the home?" I ask, scandalized. My dress doesn't cover much, but at least it covers something.

She nods, blushing prettily. "At first, I was self-conscious, but now, I don't even put it on all the time to go outside. Our home is on the outskirts, but even so, nobody pays any attention. Centaurs do not have a sense of shame in regard to their state of dress as humans do. I found it shocking at first, but you soon get used to it. In many ways, they are truer to the Goddess."

"That dress looks lovely on you," Lila adds, nodding her head toward me.

I feel self-conscious as I recall Fiona and her cruel comments. "Thank you," I say. I want to deny her complement, until I remember what Calden said at the river. There was no disgust in his eyes, nor even neutrality. There was heat and hunger, and his huge, beastly cock pushed from the sheath and leaked pre-cum over the forest floor.

Thankfully, the conversation moves on to other matters. After tea, Chastity returns to her home, where she has some chores. Lila shows me her tanning work. I have never paid much attention to the process or how the material is dyed. The day passes pleasantly until later, when Chastity returns with some herbs for Lila.

By this time, Lila has provided me with some hides and sewing supplies, so I can make my own dress. The three of us are gathered before the oak tree, while I admire the length of forest green hide that reaches to my ankles.

"I do not think it is such a good idea," Lila says, a worried pinch in her brow. "Centaurs can be very particular about what their m— um, lasses wear. Mayhap he would be accepting if you made two smaller dresses."

I am not listening, fully filled with righteous indignation that Lila's hide dress covers considerably more of her slim figure. Chastity is also better covered than me in her cloak that wraps all around her.

"There may be discipline involved," Chastity adds, looking on with a similarly worried expression. "Centaurs are proud and loving, but they also expect a strong sense of obedience from their m—ah, lasses. Now that I'm with child and Axton no longer takes the strap to my bottom, I swear the punishment is a thousand times worse."

"What could be worse than the strap?" I ask, still admiring the length of material.

Lila chuckles, and I glance up to find Chastity blushing.

"Oh, that's the worst," Lila says, patting Chastity's arm. "Gael has only done such a harsh punishment a few times when I've been particularly naughty."

"Punishment?" I demand, forgetting my manners entirely. "What is worse than a strap that might be done to a pregnant lass?" I met them only this day, and feel like I have known them all my life.

"Broth," Chastity says, her face turning bright pink. "I understand it is nutritious, yet the mere mention of him feeding me broth if I don't behave is enough to cool any querulousness."

Lila nods sympathetically. "I understand. It took me such a long time to feed from Gael. Now it is my favorite part of the day."

"It really is," Chastity agrees. "Now I'm with child, I often feed more than once."

"But what does he feed you with?" I ask, utterly confused.

Before they can answer, the sound of hooves draws our collective attention toward the forest path, where three mighty spear bearing centaurs emerge. The dark-haired centaur in the center is absolutely huge. This must be Axton, Chastity's mate. To his left is a smaller, but no less intimidating, chestnut-colored centaur who only has eyes for Lila. That must be Gael. On the right, his face darkened with anger, is Calden.

I swallow, fighting the urge to toss aside the length of hide I have stretched over my body. It is too late now, and I boldly square my shoulders. Gael glances at Calden and chuckles, seeing his thunderous expression.

"Hope," Calden says. "Did I not make the matter of your clothing clear?"

"Oh, dear," Chastity whispers. She leans in to kiss my cheek, offering me a sympathetic look before hastening to her mate, who lifts her into his arms.

Gael steps forward and similarly gathers up his mate, leaving me alone, wilting under the stern glare of the centaur I am indebted to for a moon month.

I find it hard to cling to my resolve under his censure.

"Hope?" he asks, a clear warning in his voice.

"I-I was a little chilly, milord."

He huffs out a breath in a sound not unlike the whinny of a horse. "Come, Hope. You were warned. Now I have no choice but to see to your correction."

I squeak in protest at both being lifted in the way the other centaurs lifted their mates and the threat of correction, but the moment I am in his arms, my whole body softens like I have carried a subconscious weight around with me all day. With no shame left, I press my nose into his warm, entirely human chest and breathe in his scent. How is it possible for it to be so familiar already?

My tummy is full of butterflies, and my pussy is already growing damp. I fret a little, worrying he might feel it on his arm, which to my shame, is pressed against my naked pussy.

"Don't mind it," he says. "You have been away from my musk all day. It is natural for your body to react on my return. Pity you didn't also heed my warning on matters of obedience."

I admit to being regretful now. The earlier outrage wanes under the prospect of discipline. Both Lila and Chastity did not seem to mind being disciplined. Except for the broth, which I never got to properly question them about.

On entering his home, he sets me on the floor in the center and goes to light a lamp. I stare after him, caught between worry about a spanking and admiring the play of muscles on his beautiful body. By the time he turns back, I have built myself up to a state of high anxiety.

"I... You won't feed me broth, will you?" I ask, irrationally worried about this, for unless he is a truly terrible cook, broth is not so bad. Still, Lila and Chastity's obvious abhorrence to this punishment has nevertheless unnerved me.

"Broth?" he asks, sounding as baffled about this as I am. His brows draw together.

I wring my hands. "I should like to accept my punishment, milord. Chastity mentioned her mate no longer takes the strap to her bottom if she misbehaves, on account of her being pregnant, but instead, makes her eat broth. I do not fully understand the reasons, but Lila agreed it was the worst punishment ever."

He bursts out laughing, which is confusing, but perhaps, like me, he thinks it a very odd punishment indeed.

"No, lass, I shall not feed you broth. If you can be good for me and accept your discipline, then afterward, we shall cuddle. Once you are settled, we can make some dinner. I have some venison and root vegetables, along with a generous slab of honey cake Celeste gave me as I passed through the village. She knows well how the human women love her honey cake and sent some for you."

"Oh?" I say, almost giddy at the prospect of honey cake. I was afraid that centaurs might eat…well, something strange. I am eager now to get the discipline over with so that we might cuddle and get to the cake. "I do like honey cake." A flush creeps up my cheeks, and slight dampness begins to gather between my thighs.

CHAPTER EIGHT

Calden

The women have been gossiping, it would seem.

The whole day I have been out on patrol, all I could think about was getting home and seeing how Hope had gotten on. Then I find her draping hide over herself like she is testing out the design of a new dress. Still, this does not displease me. A little rebellion is to be expected, anticipated even. My musk has a potent effect on her, and she cannot help but respond. She needs things from me, but she is too new to understand what.

"Fold the material and put it on the shelf, Hope," I say, getting my amusement at her mischief under control. Mayhap I will have words with Gael and Axton tomorrow about what their sweet mates were up to, filling Hope's head with tales of feeding, and they might both be getting broth. It will make them think twice before wagging their tongues again.

Eyes wide, she is swift to do my bidding. Her movements hold grace, for all she is a little nervous. With her back to me, I have leave to inspect her lush curves poorly hidden under the hide dress. My cock, already hard and eager at her sight and scent, leaks a long thread of pre-cum.

I shudder, steeling myself to put my hands on her for discipline, which will surely be a test.

Slipping my satchel over my shoulder, I take the things out for supper, along with the cake, and place them on the side before hanging the bag beside the door.

When I turn back, I find Hope watching me. Her eyes dart to meet mine. It does not escape my notice that she was staring at my cock, which flexes and spits a blob of pre-cum as though to entice further study.

"I think it might be best if you were to remain unclothed whilst in the home," I say. "Mayhap it will be the quickest way to purge you of these human ideas of shame."

She swallows. "Naked?"

"Indeed, lass." The more I think about this, the more I decide that this is the best course to take. She needs to be handled, to become used to me in all ways.

"Come," I say, making an upward motion with my fingers. "I have seen you before, lass. There is a hook beside the door. Going forward, you may slip your dress on before we go out and hang it upon the hook the moment you return."

She blushes to the roots of her hair.

I narrow my eyes.

She heaves a breath, setting her beautiful plump tits quivering, and reaches for the ties.

I offer a silent prayer that I might find restraint from plowing her untried cunt with my beastly cock. Her lush body emerging from the covering makes my mouth water, and my cock grows longer and harder still. "Good girl," I say approvingly as she nibbles on her lower lips and turns toward me. "Place it on the hook beside my satchel, then we shall get your discipline out of the way."

Hastening to the door, she must rise to her tiptoes to reach the hook, giving me a glorious view of her plump ass kissed by her long auburn hair. She starts when I trot over to her, and because I cannot help myself, I pick her up and carry her to the table.

"Can you see the beam, Hope?"

She nods.

"Place your feet on it and bend over the table, like a good girl."

Hope

"Oh!" I squeak out, my eyes darting between Calden and the table.

He lowers me slowly, giving me time to get my feet on the bar and bend myself forward. Goodness, it is improper and unseemly in every way to be spread out over the table before him.

"There, woman," he says, making me start when his big hands settle against my hips. His hooves thud against the compacted earth floor as he moves further behind me, nudging his big body against the cheeks of my ass. "Put your fingers into the two grooves above you on the table."

Arms stretched up, I find the grooves.

"Now, open your legs a little way for me."

When he steps back, I throw a worried look over my shoulder, thinking I must have heard him wrong.

His eyes narrow, and he taps my hip. "Open up. I do not want to use the strap, but if there is any mischief in this, I will have no choice."

I snap my head back around. With his hands bracing my hips, I ease my feet apart. My tummy clenches, and a trickle of arousal slides down my inner thighs to complete my humiliation.

He stills, and I know he has seen it and possibly scented it. I'm about to be spanked. He has very big hands, and I'm certain it will hurt. Why am I aroused?

Like I have a target on my shame, one of his hands skims down over my ass and touches the wetness, spreading it a little. His fingers are against my skin, and all I can think about is them moving closer to where I need them most. It has been so long since I experienced genuine arousal, the feeling is foreign to me. Yet the more I think about where his fingers are and the sweet relief that might be mine if only he would move them, the greater my arousal grows. I become convinced that I might come if I could press my legs together.

Calden's hands shift again, thumbs pressing into the flesh between my thighs, palms, and fingers against my ass…and then he lifts and presses me a little deeper into the wood, his beastly body touching my ass. I must bite my lower lip to stifle a groan. He shifts again, nudging me against the unforgiving wood of the table, making my breasts slide against the surface and setting me aflame.

"That's perfect," he says.

Hearing the unmistakable splat of fluid hitting the hut floor, my pussy clenches. For an alarming moment, I fear it was me, but as his rich scent saturates the air, I realize his cock has dripped pre-cum, and everything turns a little fuzzy.

"Breathe, Hope," he says.

Only all I can think about is how his cock looks when it forces from the sheath, the impossible length and girth, how much I want it, although it would surely not fit.

The sharp crack, as his palm connects with my ass, is shocking, and I gasp. Another spank follows straight after, and I can't hold in my needy moan this time.

"Good girl," he says, big palm lifting and connecting again. "Relax for me, submit to your discipline."

I don't have a choice. Everything is cross connecting in my brain, and I can't work out what or why. The rise and fall of his hand, the sharp sting, the increasing pain, the way I clench deep inside my pussy, the way I weep with need until it smears my thighs and I'm sure some of it must have dripped to the floor. Even that arouses me. The sheer debauchery of being bent over like this, naked, submitting to this beastly male, is hedonistic torture that demands relief.

I don't want him to stop.

No, I want more and become convinced that I will splinter into rapture with just a few more of those maddening spanks.

He stops.

I burst out crying, frustrated beyond belief at being denied.

"My sweet Hope," he says. Gathering my limp, sobbing body, he carries me through to his bedchamber and lies down, placing me against him. Strong arms wrap around me. My feet and legs tangle against his beastly ones as my aching breasts press against his hair roughened human chest.

I fidget and fret, yet he holds me tighter.

"Settle, love. It is done now. You are forgiven. A centaur is tolerant of much, but in matters of his charge, he expects obedience. You are mine for one moon month. You will accept my touch and my right that I might look upon your lovely form and gain pleasure from it. Never fear that I shall do more than that. I can no more help my reaction than you can, but don't mind it."

I sob harder, cling tighter, surreptitiously pressing my lips to his chest. I don't fear that he might force his attention upon me. Worse, I fear that he will not.

"I don't understand," I say. I no longer have shame, rubbing my hard nipples against Calden's chest. My thighs are coated with the evidence of arousal, and I don't even care.

"Hush, love. You have gotten yourself all overwrought. Do you want me to make you come?"

"I—No!" Even as I voice my stringent denial, I part my thighs and press my pussy against his beastly body, soaking him, trying to ease this terrible pressure.

He chuckles, his big hand cupping my hot ass possessively. "Get yourself off if you need to. You will feel better afterward."

"Oh!" I can't stop grinding my pussy against him, moaning wildly as his silken pelt catches against my swollen clit.

"Good girl, that's it. What a filthy, wonderful creature you are."

I rub and grind against him, even this light relief feeling good, and I'm rising, lifting at lightning speed toward climax.

I come and it shatters me; relief and heat rushing through me as my pussy convulses over nothing, seeming to stretch and open, gushing a flood. He holds me through the aftermath, stroking his fingers through my hair and all over me. All the tension abandons me, and I relax into him, lashes fluttering closed. Goddess, it has been so long since I felt relief.

Only now do I reconcile what I just did, realizing how my thigh is wrapped over his beastly body. Goodness, what was I thinking? I pull away, but his hand clamps against my ass, holding it in place.

"Stay where you are. It feels nice, does it not?"

Suddenly shy, I press my nose into his chest and nod. I admit, his coat is silken soft against my naked skin…and warm. I curl my cold toes under his warm body.

He chuckles. "There, you have had your way with me, come all over me, and now you are using me as a toe warmer."

I giggle.

He laughs again, a deep, resonate sound that vibrates under my cheek. I have no shame and am scandalous in my behavior. "You are very warm," I say. "I don't want to move. I-I'm sorry about that."

"Shameless hussy, you are not," he counters, and I hear the smile in his voice.

"Really I'm not," I agree. I like this, the strange burgeoning warmth in my chest, his hands upon me, and his scent filling my lungs. I lift my head. "Was there any honey cake?"

He huffs. "Honey cake. If you are hungry, I shall make some

proper dinner and you can have the honey cake after."

And even in this, I find an unexpected sense of being cared for in ways I have not been for so very long. Karl... I do not wish to sully the moment with his name, but I must acknowledge that it was I who ensured food was on the table. Not once did he trouble himself to see that I was fed.

Calden rises, his immense strength apparent when he picks me up at the same time. Not seeming to mind that I have made a little mess, he carries me to the big wooden table where I so recently felt the sting of his hand. Here, I sit and help him prepare the dinner, although he assuredly does the lion's share of the task. All the while, I watch him through new eyes. I am captivated by him, his ways, his fine, powerful body, and his thick cock that I openly study every time he turns away. True to his word, and although he must be in considerable discomfort, he does not pressure me to offer him relief. Although I cannot work out how I might, I know only that I am willing.

Perhaps more than willing.

I have been acquainted with him little more than a day, but as we share supper companionably, for it is now late, I feel as though I have known him all my life.

One moon month seemed like a high price when he first brought me here. Now, upon reflection, it does not seem like nearly enough.

CHAPTER NINE

Hope

Our days fall into a pattern. Of a day, I sit in the garden before his home, sewing. I once worked on fancy silk or fine wool gowns, but now, the material is hide and leather. The skills are new, but I enjoy the challenge and soon gain proficiency. Some days, I join Lila and work on my sewing, chatting as she goes about her hide preparations. I have even learned a little of the skill. Most days, we have tea and Chastity joins us.

It dawns upon me that this is not the feeling of being in debt.

Calden returns of an evening. We make supper together and sleep snuggled on his huge bed.

I don't hesitate to remove my dress anymore. In truth, I cannot wait for Calden to shut the door so I might strip the cursed garment off. I love his eyes upon me, although my mind still battles with the notion that this is taboo. I dedicate much time to wondering how it might be with a centaur as a mate.

As time goes by, I notice a change in me. I fluctuate between loving, joyful obedience and a churlish frustration that he does not touch me as I need. Often, I want to test him, to disobey him so that he might put me over the table again and spank me until I can let go of my cursed sense of propriety and rub my wet pussy against him to find relief.

Almost like he senses when I am up to mischief, he becomes eminently reasonable, saying my behavior is natural or understandable.

He does not spank me again.

I really wish he would.

The worst part of this is the constant ache in both my pussy and my breasts. I cannot tell whether I have gotten bigger in the hip, but my breasts are unnaturally swollen.

This evening when I enter the hut, Calden, having collected me from Lila's home, where I was helping her with some tanning, I cannot wait to tear my dress off. My breasts are extremely sensitive, bordering upon painful. Calden, who has become attuned to every nuance of my behavior, narrows his eyes on me.

"Something troubling you, lass?"

"No, milord," I squeak out, probably looking guilty.

"Hmm," he says, but then he turns away to light the stocked fire, and I see how he limps.

Forgetting all about myself, I hasten over to him. "Calden?" I press my hand to his flank. I do not touch the beastly part of him often…other than warming my toes of a night, which has become a source of great amusement for him.

He shudders at my gentle touch and stills, turning to look back at me. My eyes lower, and my gaze is drawn to where his cock begins to emerge from the sheath.

"Bear claw," he says, drawing my attention back to his face. "They plunged deep, but thankfully, he did not rake my hide when I kicked the bastard away."

The coldness in his expression makes me start. I rarely consider that side of him, the warrior who Chastity and Lila talk about. Now, I have an image of his powerful hind legs sending the bear who dared to strike him flying.

"I did not know bears attacked centaurs," I say, and not taking my hand away, for he has not asked me to, I run it over his beautiful coat, wondering where the wound is. "They must be very foolish bears."

"Shifters," he says.

"Goddess!" I swallow. I have only heard of bear shifters, but according to tales, they are considerably more ferocious and larger than a real bear. A sense of tenderness wells up inside me for this male, who took me into his moon debt. "May I tend you?" I ask.

"Let me light the fire first, lass," he says. "Then you may check if there is aught you can do. It is sore, but centaurs heal swiftly." Turning, he bends and lights the fire, blowing onto the flames until the kindling catches. Soon, there is a crackle as the wood takes, and smoke rises up the chimney.

My eyes roam over his body, which I am often shy to study. For the first time, I notice a fine crisscross of lines—old battle scars. I recall once again how he took the raiders down, efficiently and deadly. He is a warrior, and how easily I forget this when he treats me with such care and attention.

I feel like I have been cast adrift with no shore in sight.

I wonder what will become of me at the end of my moon month.

I wonder about this debt I have done naught to repay.

The air seems to charge between us as he rises and turns, revealing four distinct blood trails from deep puncture wounds. Despite his comment to the contrary, they have raked his hindquarters some.

I burst into tears.

"There, Hope," he says, and stepping over, gathers me up.

"Oh! Do not pick me up. Why do you pick me up when you are wounded? I cannot believe you would do such a thing when you should be resting!"

He sets me up on the table, as is customary of an evening.

"Sweet Hope," he says, brushing hair back from my cheeks. "I have already said the wound is not deadly."

"There is a great deal between no injury and death," I point out, crying piteously, which makes no sense, given I am not even injured. "Please turn so I might check you."

He sighs. "You are getting yourself overwrought for nothing, lass."

Only it's not nothing, and everything gathers together into a great ball of misery inside me. I like it here. I enjoy my days with Lila and having tea with Chastity, who is yet a few months from having her child. I want to be here when it is born. I cannot abide the thought of leaving, of Calden taking pleasure with a centaur lass, or worse, a human lass, which doesn't make any sense.

I sniff and gently press around the wound. "I am so confused," I say. "Please may I get water and a cloth so I might at least tend you?"

He moves off, and I miss him, even though he is only a short distance away, putting water on to heat and gathering a cloth and jar from the shelves to my left. He returns them to the table before filling a bowl with hot steaming water.

When he turns again, I steel myself and carefully apply the wrung cloth to the flesh around the wound, cleaning up the bloodstains. He remains quiet. There is an intimacy to the moment, one I like, despite my sadness at seeing his beautiful body hurt. Once the flesh around the wound is clean, I open the jar and dab a little of the pale cream over the injury.

I put the cloth back into the bowl, wishing for a high chair like Lila has so that I might reach the table on my own and disliking how it keeps me trapped. Better if I could be the one tidying up these things before making him supper while he rests. He turns back to me, making me feel shy, for I see him in a new light.

Cupping my cheek, he tips my face, forcing me to meet his gaze. He is so handsome, his beautiful snow-white hair a cloud around his face, his cheekbones sharp, and his jaw strong. His lips are thin but mobile when he smiles. I believe in that instant he must have every female in the village flustered and breathless when he turns his charm upon them.

"Thank you, Hope," he says, then his head lowers, and my breath catches, eyes fluttering in confusion and delight as he presses his lips to mine.

The kiss is warm, soft, and too brief. He moves away, gathering the things and taking them over to the side. My lips tingle where he touched them, and my tummy is full of nerves. I feel like everything I might want, wish, and hope for remains tantalizingly just out of reach.

He returns to the table, bringing the food over for me to help prepare. I complete the task quietly, but I am thinking of ways I might better make my place here. Perhaps if I were more helpful, he might view me favorably. "Do you think I might have a step?" I ask.

He pauses where he is carving a crusty loaf into thick slices. "A step?"

I point toward the floor before me. "Yes, a step so I can get up and down from the table." I'm thinking about how a step might lead Calden toward thinking about a chair. If he ordered a chair commissioned for me, that would mean he wanted me to stay, at least I think it would. Only now I am floundering when he just stares at me. "I could tuck it under the table out of the way when I wasn't using it. It would not trouble you. I might even be able to make something myself..." I trail off, nervous under his thunderous glare.

"No," he says firmly, going back to his bread, slicing it with a vigor that makes me worry I have angered him, although I've no idea how.

Perhaps he doesn't wish me to be comfortable. Perhaps he is counting the days until this moon month is over, when he can go back to his former life without a nuisance under his feet that he must carry everywhere because he thinks me helpless.

Feeling my chagrin rise, I glare back at him. "Lila has a seat."

He slams the knife down against the board. "What were you doing in Lila's house?"

"I go in there most days," I say, my temper rising now in response. I'm confused as to why this would be an issue.

"Well, I think you shouldn't be going in her house. Perhaps you should be staying at home from now on. Who knows what mischief you might come across? I told Gael plainly that he was to ensure Lila knew as much. The brat will likely be getting her bottom tanned for her mischief."

"What? That is the most unreasonable thing I have ever heard!" I say, voice rising with my ire. "You cannot punish her for being hospitable!"

"Well," he says, putting aside the bread and rounding on me in a way that sets my heart thudding and my stupid, traitorous body flushing in response. "Whether she is punished is determined by Gael, not you, Hope. Mayhap when I tell him how I expressly forbid it, he will do far worse than take the strap to her bottom."

My chest heaves as I think about the dreaded broth, although I am still to discover how this can possibly be worse than a strap applied to her bottom. "The broth?" I whisper, hardly daring to put this extreme punishment to words.

At the mention of broth, his mood shifts, lips forming a lazy smirk, even as he homes in on me, insinuating himself between my thighs, forcing my legs wide open to accommodate him, making me aware of his rich musky scent and the warmth coming from his big, powerful body. My nipples peak painfully hard, and my chest rises and falls unsteadily, drawing his attention.

His hands settle against my waist, and he nudges against me, forcing me to lean back, lest my swollen breasts touch his chest. Eyes lowering, he slowly lifts his right hand to cup my breast.

"Beautiful," he murmurs, hefting the weight in his big hand. I whimper, finding relief from the ache in being handled thus, and his brows draw together. "Are they sore, Hope?" Now he cups both sides, pressing them together, eyes turning hooded.

Hearing a distinct splat, I swallow. Goddess, he is... No, I cannot think about that.

"Hmm," he says as he continues to fondle me. "Your pretty tits are all swollen, love."

I can barely swallow past the lump in my dry throat at his words and the endearment.

"They are a little sore, milord."

"How long has this been happening?" he demands, the pad of his thumb brushing back and forth across the distended peak of my nipple, drawing a needy, desperate whimper from my lips. I can feel my pussy growing hot and slick and begin to fret. "How long, Hope?"

"A few days, milord."

He doesn't correct my use of the title. No, he is near mesmerized by my breasts.

"These tits are a fucking test," he says, voice rough as though he is in pain. Another distinct splat follows. He groans and squeezes them roughly.

"Oh!"

His eyes are on mine as he does it again. "Tell me how they feel."

"I—" Goodness, I cannot think straight when he begins to tug the nipples in time with his rough squeezing. My pussy is making a mess all over the table. "Goddess! They ache. They are sore and swollen. They feel very full!"

Nostrils flared, he takes his hands away instantly. "This is perfectly natural," he says, but there is a harsh edge to his voice, and his cheeks are as flushed as mine. The heavy splats seem to rain upon the compacted earth floor constantly.

"I-I'm not very hungry. I-I think I might need to take to bed early."

"You need to be saddled," he says before he abruptly picks me up and walks through to the bedchamber.

"S-saddled?" I murmur, already feeling better as he turns and lies down, arranging me against him.

"A figure of speech," he says soothingly. "Do not mind it."

Only I do mind it, for it feels like my not knowing what it means is further evidence of how I am not part of the herd but an outsider. He will not even let me have a stool to reach the table. I shall never be a part.

I fight. He does not let me go.

"Bad enough you are not having supper, but you will be good and still for me, or you will feel my palm against your bottom."

His words become a catalyst, and I arch up, determined not to obey him under any circumstance.

I am tipped over onto my belly, pinned with a big hand to my back, and spanked sharply against my ass.

"I shall not be good," I say, mustering all my rebellion into fighting for freedom, fully prepared to abandon my moon debt and flee the village should he let me up, even knowing that is ridiculous, given it is dark and I do not know the way back to my former home.

"I hope very much that you shall not," he snarls back, landing further sound spanks against my ass and subduing me with ease. "For I very much enjoy the way your pretty, plump ass jiggles under my palm, how pink it turns in the lamplight, how the rich scent of your naughty, needy pussy saturates the air. Do you need to get off, love? Is that what the problem is? I saw the mess you left on the table. Such a filthy lass, aroused by my rough handling of her tits, probably thinking about me touching your slick pussy or imagining rubbing yourself all over my coat like you did last time, using me for your pleasure."

"No!" I wail, but I am thinking all of that and more—how his cock must be hard and fully extended from the sheath, how he was similarly making a mess while he handled my breasts roughly.

He stops abruptly, dragging me into his arms, pressing my cheek to his chest, and gentling his hands. A soft pelt is drawn over my body, cocooning the two of us together.

My chest heaves, and my breasts quiver with every shuddering breath. My pussy, breasts, and ass throb. I want to get myself off, exactly as he described, but fierce pride and defiance win out.

"No then," he says. "If that is not what you wish, then we shall take our rest, and in the morning, we shall see if you can behave. Perhaps I might need to start applying the strap to calm your mischief."

I huff out a breath, heart pounding and not at all ready for sleep. I'm hungry, but not even the honey cake that rests under a waxed cloth holds any appeal to me. As if to further charge my ire, I soon hear his breathing even out.

My temper implodes. Calden has battled with a bear today. He is gravely wounded for all he made light of it. I feel bad, although I try to reason that I should not.

I pet his warm body and sneak a kiss against his chest. My poor pussy is drenched, swollen, and needy, my breasts sensitive to the point of distraction. My ass, cupped in his big hand, is hot and achy.

Yet I definitely want to come.

My cheeks heat just thinking about rubbing myself against him shamelessly like I did last time.

I look up at him through my lashes, seeing his eyes closed.

Maybe I can relieve one of these aches and the stern centaur won't know?

CHAPTER TEN

Hope

Carefully, oh so carefully, I shift, easing away a tiny amount so that my hand can slip down.

He stirs, and I sneak another kiss, which seems to calm him, while my fingers skitter over my belly until they reach the slick folds of my pussy. Goodness, I am drenched. I bite my lip at the first tentative touch. Even pressing my fingertips over my swollen clit feels good. I shift my knee, opening my legs around the thick girth of his body. It is not unusual for me to wake up wrapped around him, with my pussy nestled against his beastly chest.

Opening myself before him is lewd and improper, but as I am coming to discover, centaurs find such behavior entirely normal. Still, I cannot help the heat that rises in my cheeks as I consider what I do, how my fingers lightly circle my clit as I lie in the arms of a proud centaur warrior. I want to come with a desperation that consumes me. Only I want him to do it, I realize. I want his big hands to move lower, to dip between the cheeks of my ass and explore my wet folds. My fingers rub a little quicker, making wet sticky noises that sound loud and shameful in the flickering lamplight as it burns down.

Then the lamp fails, and the room is plunged into darkness that emphasizes my quickening breath and the sounds of my busy fingers, yet still, I cannot stop. My breasts quiver against Calden's chest, and I move a little, rubbing my peaked nipples against his skin.

"What is this about?"

I freeze at his deep, rumbly voice next to my ear.

He stretches, hand tightening on my ass. I glance up, seeing his eyes shining in the darkness as he looks down at me. Hand skimming over my hip, he plucks my fingers from my pussy…and brings them to his lips.

I gasp as he opens his mouth and sucks on my sticky fingers, his tongue swirling over them. My tummy clenches at the sight, mind turning to a vision of him parting my thighs and taking from the source. My pussy throbs with need, but not only my pussy, for my breasts also pulse with a dreadful pressure that never finds relief.

I whimper.

He pulls my fingers from his mouth and stares at me through the gloom. "What troubles you, Hope?" I see his lips tug up. "Do you need me to pretend to be asleep so you might carry on?"

"I-I do not, milord. I was just—" I have no idea where I am going with this or how I might save face, given what he caught me doing and further has just tasted on my fingers. Then my poor swollen breasts and hard nipples brush up against his chest, and I cannot hide my whimper.

"What was that?"

"Nothing!" My cheeks heat as I try not to give myself away by touching or glancing toward my poor sore breasts.

"It was assuredly not nothing," he says, jaw locked, reminding me that there is a stern version of Calden that expects obedience in all things. "Tell me what is wrong this instant."

My lashes lower, and my cheeks heat. "My breasts are always sore. I can hardly bear to touch them sometimes."

His nostrils flare. "Show me."

With no option to avoid this now that I have admitted to the situation, I roll onto my back and push the soft pelt away.

Face implacable, he cups the nearest breast, squeezing gently. Frowning, he rubs his thumb over the stiffly peaked nipple. "You are Goddess blessed, as I am," he says cryptically. "Do you need me to help you?"

"H-how?" I wonder if he has aught in one of his jars that might ease the ache.

His answer is to heave me up the bed until his head is level with my breast. "There, rest my Hope. Let your centaur take care of this. This is all perfectly acceptable and natural. You are not to fret about it."

Sermon delivered, he leans his head down, latches on the nearest nipple, and begins to suck.

The shock punches the air from my lungs. I gasp and squirm, but he clamps an arm around my waist and tightens until I have nowhere to go. He sucks light and fast before suddenly sucking deeply... "Oh god!"

My clit sparks to life, throbbing in time with his attention. My fingers find his hair as I am arrested by the intimacy of the moment. The weak moonlight spills in from the small kitchen window onto the main living room. He did not pull the curtain across when he brought me here, and there is just enough light for me to make out the strong lines of his face.

His sucking turns gentle again, and he laps at the stiff nipple with his tongue before sucking again. Everything is swirling together. I want to come. I don't care if it is shameful to do it in front of him anymore. All the nerves in my nipples are brought to aching life, and they find an echo deep in my pussy.

Only I am trapped and cannot do aught about my needs.

And my breast doesn't ache anymore, at least not in the same way.

His sucking slows, much to my frustration, because even though it makes me needy, I don't want him to stop. But he does stop, and his breathing evens out. Goddess, has he fallen asleep?

"Oh, you have made it worse," I mutter, no longer caring that I sound churlish, and further, he has been battling with bear shifters and is wounded and doubtless needs his sleep.

His eyes pop open, and he sucks vigorously, on the cusp of pain, before his lips slip off, leaving my nipple throbbing in a way that inflames my needs all over again.

"You are not resting," he says.

"I—" Goodness, is he taunting me or clueless? "The other side."

He goes to work, humming as he tends to me, drawing me closer to him, and my thighs open around him so that my wet pussy is pressed all over his abs.

And so begins a night of torment, where he falls asleep, periodically sucking my breasts, and I grind my pussy against him. I try telling myself that he needs rest and that I am uncharitable and unreasonable in every way to want more. But my clit feels engorged to twice the normal size and sensitive beyond belief. My pussy is open and so wet, it saturates the tops of my thighs down to the bed.

Tired and irritable, I doze only to be woken up time and time again when he begins to suckle one breast or the other while I grind my wet pussy all over him.

Only it is never quite enough to give me relief.

I am beyond frustrated as dawn begins to break and the room is cast into shades of gray. His lips have popped off, but I am desperate for the attention of his mouth and find myself surreptitiously presenting my breast to his lips, even as I begin grinding my poor swollen clit against him.

He suddenly sucks sharply, and I am so close to climaxing that I cannot help a breathy groan.

Then my eyes lower, and I realize he is staring back at me.

His lips pop off yet again, and his eyes narrow. "Little wonder you are so surly of a morning."

"I-I'm sorry," I say, nearly close to tears with my frustration. "I don't know what came over me."

"A perfectly natural reaction. Is your pussy needy? Get yourself off if you need to. I don't mind."

"I'm just overtired," I say, questioning whether I am witless to even pretend.

His eyes narrow in a most alarming way. "Are you lying, my sweet little human? We have discussed this before."

"I-I do need to come."

"Go ahead, then. You have already made a great mess all over me. Rub your pussy against me like you did last time."

Oh, why can't he do it? Why must I be the one to do this, and in such an unseemly way? My face heats. "I can't. Not while you are watching."

He sighs heavily. "This is only your human sensibilities making you think this is wrong. Nothing could be more natural than to pleasure yourself. Open your legs wider." His big hand cups my ass, making me all fluttery in my tummy. "Good girl. We shall clean up this mess you have made after. There is no hope for it now. I will suck your tits to calm you again while you do this." Taking my hand, he guides it down to my pussy and presses it into the slick folds. I shudder, almost able to imagine he is the one doing it as he guides my hand up and down. "Does that feel good?"

I nod slowly.

Lips rising in a smirk, he returns his hand to my ass as he tends to my breasts, but I am so close now that it doesn't matter. As he stares back at me, I stare down at him, watching his tongue swirl around my stiff nipple before he sucks it deep into his mouth in sharp rhythmic tugs that bring sweet relief to their fullness. My mouth opens on a wild moan as all the sensations clash, the vision of this powerful male, my busy fingers, the sticky sounds as I strum my clit, and the sweet blissful rising of nerves tingling.

The wave of bliss and relief crashes over me as I come. Mumbled cries pour from my lips, my hips jerking, my whole body spasming with joy.

Only no sooner have I finished twitching and gasping than I want to come again. Snatching my fingers away from my pussy, I burst out crying. "Oh! I think I have made myself feel worse!"

"There, Hope." Calden shifts upward, holding me close to his chest, cuddling me through my storm of tears. "You are having a hard time of it, my love. You are aroused all the time and uncomfortable. You are fighting the Goddess' will. Let yourself relax into it. Do whatever feels natural."

"I still want to come! And…and I am obsessed with your cock!" There, I have admitted my sinful thoughts.

He kicks out his back legs, dislodging the furs, and I see how his thick cock has pushed fully from the sheath, how the sticky pre-cum pools around the black tip and soaks the bedding. "It is only a cock," he says. "All beasts and men have one."

"You're not a beast," I say, although I'm guilty of thinking of him thusly many times, and now that brings me shame.

"Compared to you, I am." He runs his fingers down my cheek. "Would you like me to tend to your pussy? My poor love, I'm certain you would feel better if I cleaned you all up." He nuzzles the side of my breast before drawing the peaked nipple into his mouth and suckling it, once, twice before stopping. "But perhaps you are not ready for that."

He has mentioned my readiness before, and I am fed up with him telling me I'm not ready all the time.

He shifts, and my eyes go to his huge cock. My pussy throbs, and I lick my lips.

"Try to sleep, little human, or you will be naughty in the morning and I'll have no choice but to saddle you and take the strap to your bottom. If you could take my goodness into you, it would go a long way to soothing you. You had no supper and barely touched it yesterday evening. My body is merely reacting to your needs."

My mind spins as I try to process everything he said. Saddling? His goodness? How is he reacting to my needs?

"I don't want food," I say honestly. Nothing appeals to me, not even honey cake. My eyes are drawn once more to his flexing cock, and my tummy rumbles loudly.

"Go ahead," he says. "There is nothing between us that is wrong before the Goddess. You have gifted me. It is entirely natural that I should likewise gift you."

My eyes are everywhere, yet I see nothing. Is he…is he talking about his cock and the thick pre-cum leaking from the tip? I send a furtive glance his way. "You want me to…ah…to…" I swallow and gesture toward his cock.

"Of course. I'm yours, sweet little human. You are not eating and sleeping poorly. My balls are fit to bursting, and my cock weeps all the time. It only wants to serve you."

Goodness!

I move, half tumbling over him in my haste, mouth already watering, ravenous and determined. "How?" I ask in a hushed whisper, eyes darting from my prize to his face, seeing the raw desperation there. He needs this, I realize, just as I needed him to tend to me. I look back, daunted by his immense length and girth. In the moonlight, I can see how heavy and swollen his balls are. He must be in pain!

"Do what feels natural, Hope. You will not harm me, although I

75

must warn you that I am close. Just the feel of your small hands and lips upon me will likely send me over the edge."

As I tentatively cup his balls, he rolls, pushing out his hind leg, exposing himself fully to me. He makes a sound not unlike a whinny of a horse.

"Do they hurt?" I ask, my eyes flashing to meet his through the gloom.

"Goddess, yes, all the time. They are so heavy and swollen with seed. It is hard for a centaur to address such matters and further feels wrong to seek another for relief when it is all for you."

I fondle his poor swollen balls gently, stilling when he shifts, spreading his stifle and kicking out his top leg further so that I might fully get to him. "I am close to fucking bursting," he says, voice harsh.

As I lift his great cock in both hands, it flexes, and he moans piteously. A thick gush spills from the tip, covering my hands.

Goodness!

He is throbbing, his balls swollen and tight. He said that I should do whatever was natural, and it is the most natural thing to lower my head and lick. I am shocked as the spicy taste explodes across my tongue. I lap and suck, taking it into my belly. Gently cupping his heavy balls, I stroke my other hand over the thick length, hoping for more.

He moans again, and another small gush is my reward. I lick and suck it all up, feeling my pussy begin to throb as I realize what I am doing, how I am on my knees handling a centaur's cock, touching, licking, and greedily sucking all the goodness up. Using both hands to work the length, I open my mouth as wide as possible to accommodate the flared tip, not wanting to lose any. My hands move faster, and I become a little dizzy with need, empowered to be touching this powerful male thusly. Craving more, I get my tongue deep into the slit. I hum around the head as his fingers spear my hair.

"What a beautiful vision," he says, and I glance up to find him watching me tend to him, his eyes hooded with pleasure. "I have so much to give you, love. It is my duty to keep your pretty, plump body perfect for me, to care for you. Take what you need."

I glide my hands from the root to the tip, eager for the next gush.

"So pretty, love. Do you need more? Do you need me to come so I might fill you all up?"

I groan around his cock. I do, I really do, boldly cupping his balls and feeling how much more swollen they are.

He groans deeply, and his balls tighten before a great gush of cum pours down my throat. It spills out over my chin as I gulp greedily, stroking his length as best as I can, fondling his straining balls for more, and all the while he groans with such relief that I become enraptured by the sound. My belly is full for the first time in days, but I keep sucking and licking, making sure I get every drop, coaxing his tight balls to give me more.

He groans, and another splash hits the back of my throat, the sweetest yet, and absolutely delicious.

"There, love," he says, voice roughened. "You have drained your poor centaur. Come here and let me cuddle you close."

Only I am not yet done, and I glare at him while lapping my tongue over the thick slit at the top and defiantly cupping his balls. He groans, ejecting a weaker gush.

"Oh!" I am snatched up from my prize.

"My sweet, greedy love. You have stuffed yourself silly."

Gathered in his arms, I am still licking cum from my fingers as I sigh contentedly.

He chuckles. "Better now?"

"Much. I feel sleepy." I snuggle in close, feeling better than I have in many days. "I didn't know."

"How could you?" he says. "You are yet new to centaur ways. Goddess have mercy. My balls are still straining to give you more."

He scoops a splash of his cum from my breast and offers it to my lips.

Eagerly, I lap his fingers clean, but my eyes have strayed to his cock. It has gone down a little but not completely, the flared tip still exposed from the sheath. "I want some more." My own words shock me.

"Tomorrow, love."

I go to protest, but suddenly, I feel funny, tingly, and urgent between my legs. "Oh!" I press my palm to my lower belly, feeling a strong clench low in my womb.

My hands are snatched away, and Calden holds me closer. "Relax into it, Hope." He presses a kiss to my forehead, just as a flush passes through my body and my pussy contracts.

A moan erupts from my mouth as waves of white-hot bliss course through my body. I'm coming, convulsing, pussy clenching and relaxing and clenching again as I arch up against him. He seems to know what I need, and his lips latch onto my breast, sucking sharply and deeply, which just makes all pleasure rippling through me twice as intense. I cling to him, losing all sense of shame, and thrust my breasts into his face as my body splinters into waves of pleasure.

CHAPTER ELEVEN

Hope

The curtain to the bedchamber is only half drawn when I wake the next day, and sunlight is streaming through the kitchen window, making a dappled pattern over the compacted floor of the main living room.

Calden is long gone, and his home is quiet. My thoughts flit through the events of last eve. I don't know what to make of it, nor the strange feelings that assault me. I cannot believe I touched him thusly and took him into my mouth. My breasts are aching, although they are not as bad as yesterday, more a good kind of achy, almost tingly, like I want him to tend to them again. Unable to help myself, my fingers skitter down my body and into the slick folds of my pussy. I feel strange there too, open and empty as this unexpected carnality rises inside me, both desperation and wonder at how it would be to join with a centaur fully.

Pushing the covers back, I rise and pad through into the main living area. My mind wants to recoil and say it is impossible, yet Lila and Chastity are testament to the fact that it is possible. Still, how would we... It all seems so awkward. Even as I acknowledge this, I must also acknowledge that it felt natural between us yesterday.

I am drawn to him.

I inch the shutters open, letting in a little light, along with the sounds of the busy village. What would my late mother have said, were she alive to see me cavorting with a centaur?

Happy, immediately comes to mind. I think she would be happy for me and would look past the differences, for we may be different species, but we are all one before the Goddess. He has called me 'my love' more than once, and every time, the lonely place in the center of my chest awakens and comes to life.

I want to hope but am afraid to. What am I to him? A woman he found in trouble. I'm quite convinced this moon debt is not a debt at all, but some noble quest on his behalf to keep me safe for a time.

I sigh.

On the sideboard, I find a pitcher of water, a bowl, and a cloth, which I am just able to reach, and clean up. After I have finished, I dress and head for the river, which always gives me a sense of peace. As I set out the front door, I find many people and centaurs about. They call greetings. "Hail, Hope!" Centaurs, I have discovered, are friendly and cheerful, yet I only have to think about Calden's terrible wound after the fight with a bear shifter to realize that all is not perfect here.

The riverbank is quiet, and I sit on the mossy ground and dip my toes in the cool water. My feelings are growing for Calden, but I must still myself, for he is not taking me as a mate. I am in his debt. I think on how Chastity and Lila came to be with their mates, how they happened upon them in danger, just as Calden happened upon me. Only in their case, they became mates. Surely if Calden wanted to mate me, he would have said so?

I'm restless. The day is pleasant, with a warmth in the air, but I do not wish for my own company, so I quit the river and take the lane to Lila's cottage. When I knock on the door, she opens and greets me with a smile that goes some way to settling my mood.

"Hail!" she says brightly. "Come on in, we were wondering where you were. We are making tea and will have the cake Celeste brought over yesterday eve. You are very late this morning."

I blush, remembering why I am later than usual this morning. Despite all the confusion in my mind, I very much hope we might have the same pleasure tonight. If this moon month is all I have with him, I do not want to waste any of it. If this truly is natural, as he says, then I want more, so that I might store these wonderful memories up.

Only this time, I will not be so reserved, nor will I deny what I want. Perhaps then he will change his mind about me and decide he needs a mate.

Chastity is busy at the table, where a prepared tray holds cake and cups ready to take outside. "How are you today?" she calls. "You have a little glow to your cheeks. How was Calden? I hear they left early. There was some trouble with the bears that they went to investigate."

"Indeed, a troubling business," Lila agrees.

"I slept a little late," I say, blushing hotter still.

Chastity smirks. "Some centaurs have a powerful effect upon a woman. There is nothing you need to worry about, given all the trauma you went through. I think sleeping in on occasion might be good for you." Gathering the tray, she heads for the door.

"Would you help me with these hides?" Lila calls. "I want to take them outside, where we can pick a nice one for Chastity's new cloak."

"Of course," I say, hurrying over. Beside the bedchamber entrance is a tall cupboard, where Lila keeps all her supplies.

"Look how pretty this color came out," Lila says, showing me a stunning green hide.

"And soft," I say, smiling as she offers it to me. It's then that I notice the curtain, which is normally drawn across her bedchamber, is open.

Lila is distracted, selecting more hides to take outside, but I am captivated by the strange assembly to the right of their bed.

What is it for?

Calden has a similar space in his room, but it is empty. I blink a few times as I try to work out what it is. It is fashioned much like a high bench, with wide, grooved troughs to each side. On top is a strangely-shaped padded section that reminds me of a saddle.

My face heats as I recall Calden's words. *"...I'll have no choice but to saddle you and take the strap to your bottom."*

Goddess! Is that how a centaur takes a human lass? Oh, I am certain it is, and further, that this is why Calden did not want me to enter Lila's home. I had forgotten all about his instruction this morning, given I was distracted and flustered after being late.

"Oh," Lila says softly, and my eyes are torn from the saddle to Lila's troubled face.

Like my eyes have a will of their own, they shift back to the assembly, only to have it snatched from my view as she snaps the curtain across.

"Sorry," I say, feeling the rudeness of me staring at something so personal and intimate.

"It is not your fault," she says, wringing her hands together. "I was told not to let you see. Please don't tell anyone. Oh, Gael will be cross and I will suffer the worst punishment ever!"

"The broth," I say, suddenly understanding what that means. My lips tug up, despite the churn in my stomach.

Her return smile is shy but soon drops, and I sense her genuine fear that I might tell on her. "It's okay," I say. "I was just curious. It was rude of me to stare."

"He doesn't want you to see it," she says.

By he, she means Calden. I'm sure she does, and the sickly sensation expands low in the pit of my belly. I smile brightly, but inside, I am crumbling and a mess. "Calden doesn't have one," I say unnecessarily.

"No." A bright stain covers her cheeks. "He does not. He has never… He does not take human lasses in that way. Gael and Axton, they both already had one for they enjoyed human maidens before Chastity and I arrived."

I swallow, but the sick feeling does not abate.

"Please don't tell anyone," she repeats, wringing her hands again. "Oh, I will be in such trouble for this."

"Do not mind it," I say, placing a hand upon her shoulder and gently squeezing it. I move away, not wanting her to notice how my hand trembles. "I shall not tell anyone. Why would I? This is obviously a natural thing between a centaur and his mate." For some centaurs. The coldness intensifies. "This hide is beautiful. I'm certain this shall make a beautiful cloak!"

My encouraging words and smile hide the sorrow unfurling inside me. Moreover, I am ashamed of my jealousy toward these two beautiful women, who have only been kind to me. They have met and been claimed by cherished mates, and I am merely an outsider.

"If you are certain you are all right," she says, although her expression suggests she is still worried. "I understand it is a shock at first. Centaurs are highly carnal creatures, and their ways can be daunting."

Only I'm no longer daunted, and even the shock has passed.

I follow Lila outside into the bright sun, where we chat and drink tea and eat cake. Inside, I'm cold, and my tummy is aflutter in an unpleasant way. He doesn't want a human woman, not in that way. He has never been with a woman before, Lila said as much. He does not want to saddle me for pleasure, nor for me to linger permanently.

He certainly doesn't want a chair for me like Lila and Chastity have. Even the mere suggestion of a stool for me to reach the table made him angry. No, it is altogether clear that Calden does not want his home changed for a woman. I am nothing but a moon debt who will be on my way.

I try to count the days I have already been here and how many are left, but they have blurred a little, perhaps more than half the moon month...perhaps more than that.

This is the cruelest, bitterest, most depressing and utterly shattering development that could be made. It is a testament to my will that I keep my tears inside and my face cheerful. As Chastity decides to leave to work on her vegetable plot, I similarly elect to go as well.

Lila watches me worriedly. "Please don't mind what happened. I can tell it has unsettled you."

"Does it... Is it difficult to be with a centaur?" I wonder why I would broach the subject when I know it shall never come to be.

She shakes her head and blushes prettily. "No," she says. "It is only pleasure, the most amazing pleasure. Not all centaurs are as loving nor respectful of the Goddess' way. I understand that I am blessed to have found this herd and not another, wickeder one."

"How so?" I ask.

"Some centaurs are wicked in the darkest, most depraved of ways," she says, voice hushed like she is fearful to mention them. "They are not gentle with their human mates, but instead take and keep them by force."

I swallow nervously. I have heard dark tales about centaurs and have been constantly surprised by how Calden and his herd did not conform to those tales.

"Axton's herd is nothing like that. You are safe here, Hope." She suddenly blushes again. "I'm not saying there wasn't some adjustment, discomfort, and confusion at first. But goodness, I would not change a thing. I love Gael, and soon, we will have a child of our own." Her hand goes to her stomach, and she rests it there with a reverent expression on her face.

"You are with child?"

She nods, smiling. "I am. It took so long. I was so worried that it might not happen at all, and jealous, though it is a weak emotion, when Chastity was with child so swiftly. I cried many nights, despairing, but now I see that sometimes, matters of love are not resolved quickly and that is okay too."

I feel like she is trying to tell me something, but I still reel from this news. My heart softens for her plight. I think about how I have always wanted a child, but how little I wanted one with Karl. Now, I would love to be with child, if only that child were Calden's, but that is a foolish wish. "I'm so thrilled for you." I reach across and take her hand. "You are blessed in every way."

"I am," she agrees. "Now, please do not mind what you saw. Never think that Calden would do something to you without your permission, and that you did not also need and want."

I dash away the stupid tears that spill down my cheeks. "I know," I say. "I have already realized as much. He is a fine male and a proud centaur. I could not pick a better being that I might be indebted to."

She hugs me, and I hug her back. I have known Lila for a short time, yet she is already dear to me. This whole village, the centaurs and their ways, their vigor for life, how joyfully they go about their chores and care for one another, it all has bewitched me. It is the finest place in all the lands, surely.

Yet it is not my place, and I know that although I promised him a moon month, I cannot stay here any longer.

Calden

"So how are things with your little moon debt?" Gael asks as we trot through the forest, spears in hand, on the morning patrol.

My right hip aches where the bear shifter buried his claws into me yesterday. I didn't want to make much of it in front of Hope, fearing she may not view the village as safe, but it aches like a bastard.

"Well enough," I say noncommittally.

He chuckles. "You're in a better mood today, not trying to rip my head off, nor are you gripping your spear shaft like it is my neck when I dare to broach the topic."

I chuckle. "Things are progressing," I say. "She finally fed last eve, although my little human had worked herself into a state before finally submitting to her needs."

"I still remember Lila," he says dryly. "It took nearly a month. Gods, how my cock and balls ached. She was so shy about it. Still, such matters cannot be rushed."

"Hope wasn't eating, which was a sure sign she was changing and needed me. I'm glad I let nature run its course, for I have been twice blessed," I say gruffly, thinking about how her plump tits had been swollen with sweet nectar.

He cuts a look my way, eyes narrowing with interest. "How so?"

"Her tits needed to be tended."

He raises both brows before his face splits into a grin. "You are indeed blessed," he says. "Very few are gifted in such a way." His eyes turn speculative. "What does it taste like?"

"Sweet," I say. "Pleasant upon the tongue. When it hit my belly, I almost fucking came. Had I not been so exhausted after the fight with the bear, I'd have had to take a dip in the lake just to steady myself."

He chuckles again. "I heard your saddle is nearly ready. When are you going to put it in place? Best not to be caught out if you are nearing that stage. Much safer if they are securely strapped in where they cannot move and hurt themselves in the heat of passion…and better for discipline time."

"I don't know," I say. "I'm not convinced she is ready. The

situation was different for you and Axton, for you already had one in place. She asked me for a step yesterday—a fucking step! Like I would gift her something so lowly." I shake my head. "The chair is ready, but it feels forward to just put it there."

"She won't know what it means," he says. "And by the time she does, she'll be happy either way."

Yet it doesn't sit right to put either the chair or the saddling station in my home until I am confident, lest I frighten my tiny human. I ordered them for her, and only her. I already know there is no other woman who might come into my life that I would want in this way. I had no interest in a mate before Hope, and should this not work out, I shall never be with another human woman again, and perhaps no centaur, either.

I swallow against a lump in my throat. "The time is not yet right," I say. "I will know when…and you might need to have words with your mate. As does Axton."

"How so?"

"I asked both Lila and Chastity not to take Hope into your homes. I found out last eve she had been inside every day."

"Lila gets excited, and doesn't rightly think things through," he says, smirking. "She has taken to your Hope and seeks only to welcome her. Still, you spoke plainly when you explained your reasons. She should be more careful. I'll need to be mindful of how I discipline her though, given she is pregnant."

My head swings around. They have been trying for a year, and they were both praying for the gift. I grin and slap him on the shoulder. "That is wonderful news."

He nods, grinning broadly. "Aye. We have been blessed." His grin turns rueful. "Shame I can't take the strap to her bottom anymore. It'll have to be the other type of punishment." He wiggles his eyebrows.

"I've heard many stories of how human mates would do anything to avoid having their daily treat. I foresee Lila being one sorry little mate," I say, not unkindly.

"It will pain me as much as it pains her, but tomorrow, she'll be enthusiastic, and I'll enjoy that as well."

We both laugh, for there is nothing better than an enthusiastic mate, as I have recently learned.

We spend the day out on patrols, and I put matters of what comes next with Hope from my mind. I was determined to go slow with her last night and worried that it was too much, too soon. Then this morning, it was hard to leave her for the patrol and my duties, ones that cannot be put on hold, even for a woman I hope will soon become my mate.

The safety of all, including Hope, transcends personal desires. Life is such, and we return home late, where the centaurs on duty greet us with a cheery hail. Separating at the village square, we head to our respective homes.

With the onset of dusk, the homes I pass emit a warm glow, and a few villagers are about, but on reaching our home, I find it to be dark. I call out to her upon entering but receive no response.

I frown. "Hope!" I search the bedchamber, sensing it is empty, even before my eyes confirm it. My stomach sinks, and turning, I exit the home. "Hope!"

Peter, a young centaur lad, is passing. "Have you seen Hope, lad?"

"No, Calden," he says. "Not since midday, when I saw her upon the lane that leads to the stables. Mayhap she was going to check upon the horses you brought back. I've caught her sneaking them a carrot on occasion." He smiles warmly, although I do not feel warm. Instead, I am ice-cold.

"Thank you, lad." I trot over to Gael's home, a sick, unwelcome feeling churning in my gut, and knock upon the door. Gael opens the door, a smile on his face. It drops on seeing me.

"Hope is not home," I say. He throws a look over his shoulder. "Do you know where Hope is, Lila?"

"I—No," she says, her pretty face turning a deathly shade of white.

"When did you last see her?"

"Lunchtime." She wrings her hands and sends a fearful look Gael's way. "I-I…"

She cannot get the words out. Something has happened, I am sure of it. "Do you know where she might have gone?"

Lila shakes her head.

There is no time for a discussion on the how or why. "It is late and growing dark," I say.

"We'll call the guard," Gael says decisively, snatching up his spear. "Bolt the door, Lila. We will talk upon this when I return."

CHAPTER TWELVE

Hope

Night is falling, and I am cold and tired when I reach the outskirts of a farmstead. A sense of danger emanates from the forest behind me, but I do not know this place, and danger is also ahead. The mare I stole from Calden's herd is conspicuous, but I cannot leave her in the woods. The haunting howls that sound in the distance set the hairs on the back of my neck prickling with unease. This forest is no place for horses or humans.

I carefully pick my way around the outskirts. The small, squat cottage emits a cherry glow, with smoke rising to the sky. I have no reason to presume these people are hostile, but I am unsettled from my flight and the reason that brought me to this moment and not ready for company. I find a likely barn full of hay close to the forest, away from the main farm building. Easing the bolt from the door, I push it open and walk my mare inside with me.

It's dark, and I can see little once the sturdy door is pushed shut, but I feel immediate relief to have a barrier between the forest and me. We both drank plentifully from the nearby stream, so although our bellies are empty of food, it will have to do. I pat my mare and gift her the last carrot from my pocket. "Good girl," I say. "I will get you a little hay to munch before we rest. This is better than the forest, hmm?"

She snorts into my hand, seeking more food. I pat her neck before relieving her of the bridle and saddle.

The situation leaves a bad taste in my mouth. I question why I would run, just as I question how I could stay. My feelings toward Calden have ever been ones of love and respect, but of late, they changed into a different, deeper kind of love.

The kind that exists between two soulmates.

Only we can't be. I am his for only a moon month, and after, he will free me of my debt. I don't even care that he is a centaur, and I, a human lass. I have come to understand that love transcends such things. Yet how can I love him if he does not also love me? Must it not be an equal and sacred commitment to create true love?

I take a handful of straw and rub down my sweet mare's coat as best I can. She whinnies softly, enjoying the attention.

I miss him.

I miss his patience and his gentleness, his firm but loving ways. He is everything I hoped for but did not receive with Karl. Maybe I should have spoken to him? Maybe he could have come to love me in time?

Only he didn't want a human lass. He doesn't even have a saddle for me, like Gael has for Lila.

I make a place for myself against the hay. I'll need to be up early, so I do not get caught here. Although where I will go after, I have yet to decide.

I'm hungry and tired from the travel.

I miss his scent surrounding me.

I miss his humor and zest for life.

I miss his touch.

I have a terrible feeling that I have made the gravest of mistakes.

Against all likelihood, I fall asleep in the barn. The cold wakes me up, and instantly, I miss the comfort and warmth from when I would nestle against Calden's body. I shiver, realizing the sun has risen and I can hear the sound of voices beyond the barn door.

"What's this about?" a male voice calls. A shot of fear races through my body. Rising, I creep over to the edge of the barn and peek through a gap in the slats. "Somebody passed this way last night."

In daylight, the ramshackle nature of the farm buildings is apparent. I spy an older, gray-haired man talking to a younger dark-haired man. I can see the family resemblance from this small distance, perhaps father and son. These are poor people whose tattered clothing and scruffy appearance tell a story.

"What are you lazy bastards doing?" a woman calls. "See to the fucking pigs."

"Someone came through, Myrtle," the older man says gruffly. "Don't like folks nosing around our business."

I have seen mere moments of these people, yet I already know they are not the people I wish to be caught by, nor do I presume they would offer me charity. My state of dress, which was acceptable in the centaur village, will surely label me as a wild woman. My eyes dart around the barn, looking for another way out. My horse, which once belonged to the raiders, flicks her ears back and forth and issues a low whinny.

"Steady, girl," I say, hurrying over to her and running my hand over the glossy coat at her throat, praying that she will be quiet. Perhaps I could slip away. There is a hatch in the side that might allow me out. I didn't want to leave the horse here. My instincts cry that these are not kind people. I reason that they must be better than the raiders and have the right to be displeased with me, given I have stolen away in their barn. Still, my best hope is to ride out. I am certain that these poor farmers do not have a horse. If I can only get outside without their notice, I can ride away hard and fast.

Heart racing, I lift the saddle from where I laid it on the old bale of straw, carefully placing it over her back. My hands shake so violently, it is all I can do not to drop it. It takes three attempts to pass the strap under her girth, where I fumble to slip the leather through the buckle. She stomps her feet, and I look back toward the door, expecting them to burst in at any moment. Carefully, so carefully, I tighten the strap before reaching for the bridle. "Good girl," I say as I ease it over her head. Outside the barn, I can hear the people of this farmstead bickering among themselves, separated from us by the sturdy barn door.

I have a wild idea to fling the door open and gallop out. Mayhap if they clear the courtyard for a moment, I can make my escape. Only they don't turn in the other direction, and to cement my doom, I hear footsteps draw close.

I fumble with my task, my hands shaking so badly that I can't make the harness comply with my needs.

"Please, Goddess, please!" I mutter under my breath, fingers clammy and clumsy.

Finally, it is in place. More shouting ensues. "Get the hounds," the woman calls. "Reckon they are hungry and can sniff any trouble out."

I hiss under my breath, mind frantic.

The voices fade. They are moving away. I have a chance, given they are sending for hounds, and I cannot afford to delay. "Good girl," I say to my mare. "We can do this. We can get away." Carefully, I lead my horse over to the barn door and open it a crack. The courtyard is empty. We need to make our escape.

Hoisting myself up into the saddle, I take the reins in my clammy hands. It is now or never. Yet the act of opening the door further so we can exit becomes a task of immense difficulties, and fear incapacitates me. I heave a breath, tighten my hands upon the reins, and reach to fling the barn door open.

It creaks loudly, setting my frayed nerves to breaking, but it is open now. My horse, sensing my fear, trots forward nervously, flicking her ears, eyes a little wild. I look right where the voices were.

Three people are gathered before an outbuilding—the older and younger man I saw earlier, along with a stout woman in similarly scruffy clothes with a grubby apron around her waist. Between them are two young lads with collars around their throats and leads held by the woman.

"Stop, thief!" the older man cries.

Fear shoots through my veins, galvanizing me into action. I squeeze my horse's belly between my thighs and flick the reins. My mare takes to flight, sensing the imminent threat as I do. My last glance back sees the woman release the lads from their leashes.

"Take the bitch down," she orders at a scream. Like a vision from a nightmare, the two pitiful young lads transform before my eyes. Where once they were human, now they are abominations, with blood-red fur and snarling slavering jaws.

My horse screams and takes off into the forest at a thunderous pace, but the hellhounds are coming.

I cling to my horse's neck, understanding that I have no control here. My horseback riding skills are fair but certainly not up to managing, and my poor girl is in a state of visceral fear. Even if I could, I am in no better state. The trees and forest flash past. The baleful howls and snarls come from behind us as the hounds make their pursuit. The pathway here is narrow, and branches whip at me as we pass by on our mad race.

I know not where we are going, only that we must go. It was late when I arrived, and I am unfamiliar with this part of the empire. A stream lies before us, and we splash through before my horse scrambles up the far bank.

The hounds are closing in, their howls sharper, louder, their snarls vicious and full of wrath.

A sob of pity escapes my throat, for my dear horse is tiring under this frantic pace. I whisper prayers, even as I curse my stupidity at fleeing the centaur village. Oh, how foolish I have been.

The hounds are gaining, one flanking us.

My prayers are not answered. The horse stumbles and goes down screaming, throwing me. Tumbling, I land in the undergrowth. The horse screams again, a terrible sound of pain. I rise but fall back as a vicious, snarling, unearthly beast bears down on me. Lips curled back, it snaps its teeth over my face.

Out of my periphery, I see my horse gain her feet. The hounds show no interest in her and focus instead upon me. The horse trots a few paces away, just as a cry comes from the forest path.

"They got the hussy!" I hear the woman, Myrtle, call, shooting urgency into my frantic state. I try to rise but snapping teeth warn me to remain in place.

"Heel," Myrtle calls, and the hounds hasten to her side and sit. I scramble up, not knowing where I will go but only that I must go somewhere. Coarse laughter is followed by the thud of approaching footfalls before strong arms surround me, picking me up and cutting short my flight. They close in.

"Got her," the younger man says. "Look at her and how she dresses. One of those simple-minded savages."

"No wonder the hounds were going wild. They recognize her scent," the older man says as I'm hauled kicking and screaming toward them. I am dropped to the ground before the hounds and Myrtle. Scooting backward, I gain my feet, only to crash into the younger man, who closes his fingers over my arms.

"Got ourselves a fine prize, Myrtle," the old man says, nodding.

"That we have, Col," she replies. "And a feisty one at that." Her arm swings. I try to dodge, but her palm cracks against the side of my face, the sound loud and shocking before the pain robs me of breath.

I taste blood, stagger, and am dragged back by the younger man.

"Omega," Col says ominously.

I shake my head, thoughts scattering and gathering. An omega? Surely not? There have been no omegas in our village as far back as records tell.

"The centaurs will pay a fine price for her kind," Myrtle adds, nodding.

No, they cannot mean Axton's herd, surely? He would not pay for omegas, would he? My lips and cheek throb, and blood pools in my mouth, but hope surges too, for I am certain that if Axton were to pay a high price for an omega, it would be so he might rescue them.

"Better get her horse, Reggie," Myrtle says. "We'll need you to ride with all haste for Grimm's outpost at the crossing."

Grimm?

"I meant no harm," I say, my voice brittle. "I got lost and sought shelter. I'm sure Axton and his herd are already looking for me."

My ruse in name-dropping is met with sharp laughter. "Better steer clear if you spot any of Axton's herd, lad. Likely Axton and his Goddess fearing herd will be looking for their lost prize. Grimm will pay us even more."

"Some centaurs are wicked in the darkest, most depraved of ways," Lila told me yesterday. *"They are not gentle with their human mates, but instead take and keep them by force."*

Suddenly, I am sure that Grimm, the centaur these wicked people are sending for, is one of the dark centaurs Lila spoke about.

CHAPTER THIRTEEN

Calden

The forests of northern Hydornia are not a safe place of a night, even for centaur. Hope has half a day head start on us, and given she took a horse, could be far away by now.

Forming parties of two or three, we separate and continue upon our chase, following well-traveled pathways and those that are not. My mind takes to wondering as we thunder down the forest paths. Why would she leave? Was she fearful of me? I berate myself for my part in this, but I am also furious with her. We have shared intimacy. We have slept together every night since I found her under attack by villainous scum. Does she think so little of my character to put herself into danger thusly?

A moon month was all I required, but even so, should she have asked me, I would have reluctantly let her go.

She does not know this area and has never left her village of Melwood. Where she intended to go and to what end is beyond my understanding, but as time passes and the sky lightens, the tender place inside of me slowly shrivels and dies. As agreed, we meet on the edge of a deep gorge with the other hunters of the valley. Gael and I are the last to arrive, and I search the crowd in the desperate hope that she might have already been found.

She has not, and a coldness sharpens inside my chest.

I trot over, my aggression prevalent in every step. "I will not return without her," I say boldly, meeting my herd leader's eyes.

"I am not asking you to," Axton replies.

His words go some way to calming the franticness clamoring inside me. "We are not yet mated," I say. "I have not yet saddled her, but I do not believe she has gone to the Goddess. Not yet." I have no proof of this. The forest teems with monsters of every kind—bears, bear shifters, wolves, and trolls. This land to the north of Hydornia is full of magical beings. A portal lies not far from here that often opens and spills all manner of creatures into the surrounding lands. So no, I have no evidence that Hope is still alive, yet I believe it is so in my heart and I will not give up.

Axton trots forward and places his hand upon my shoulder. "We will do what we must to find her," he says. "But some of our numbers must return to the village, for there is not enough protection for an extended period."

My jaw locks, and I nod once. Axton is my herd leader. I have obeyed him without question all of my life. I understand that what he says is right and true, but selfishly, I'm thinking only of myself.

"There are farms in this region," a centaur calls. "The lass might have stumbled upon them."

"Heathens, all of them," Gael says. "Many are in with Grimm, doing his bidding."

Axton turns about swiftly, his hand falling from my shoulder. "We are sure she came this way?"

"Aye," Gael says. "The horse tracks lead west. It's possible she led us wrong, seeking to disguise her trail and then doubled back, but unlikely. The paths grow steep north of the village and are not well suited to a horse. Had she abandoned the beast, it would have made its way back toward the village. Hope was in the village long enough and must know the bear shifters live to our east. She would not have gone that way either, which leaves only west or south.

"Toward Grimm," I say, fist tightening upon my spear.

Gael nods slowly. "Toward Grimm, but there are many homes between and not all of them adhere to the dark ways."

Still, most of them do. "The chance of her surviving the night on her own outside is low," I admit. "Mayhap she has holed up somewhere, perhaps an abandoned farm, of which there are many in this region."

No centaur within our herd has more than passing tolerance for Grimm. He is a bloodthirsty heathen who neither worships the Goddess nor adheres to her ways. Still, he is powerful, and his herd is significantly larger than ours. There are tales that they take women against their will. My chest tightens imagining such a fate.

Every year, Axton rides for the villages, entreating them not to offer their young girls. Still, some do, fearing Grimm's wrath, and others for the offer of coin.

It is a terrible burden to know you do not have the power to stop corruption and abuse, that all you can do is protect your own, and that you cannot liberate those who suffer in a place so close.

Grimm has his uses. He protects our lands from the ungodly creations that spill through the portal…mostly. A few do still slip through. This is not an alliance that exists between our herds, more a tolerance.

"If he takes her—"

"He won't," Axton says.

"He might," Gael says, and I'm inclined to agree with him.

"She has been blessed and responds to my scent. She is sensitive, and we all know what that means, although we do not speak of it often. Even if we did, the women wouldn't know what it meant."

"An omega," Axton says, nodding. "And I agree—if he happens upon her, or others do and realize her value, they will surely take her to him."

I note the way his knuckles turn white around the handle of his spear.

"This is my problem," I say. "It is not the problem of the whole herd. I will challenge him if he has dared to take her."

Axton's face hardens, reminding me he is the leader and why. I swallow and lower my eyes in submission.

"We are one herd," he says, voice carrying as he looks around at all of us.

Shame fills me that I dared to speak thusly to him, yet my heart is heavy at the thought that we might wage war upon Grimm, for it would mean the death of warriors and leave widows and fatherless children. Still, we are one herd, as he says. We fight together, and if necessary, we will die together.

"He will not court our wrath," Axton says, pinning me with a look. "But if he does, then he shall get it."

I meet the eyes of every centaur present, seeing the same determination upon their faces. I am humbled before the Goddess and everyone here.

"We are one herd," Gael repeats before the other centaurs take up the call.

Finally, Axton turns toward me.

"We are one herd," I agree.

Hope

My horse is swiftly captured by Reggie, and the young lad takes off into the forest, while my cruel new master and mistress take command of me. Col fists me by the arm. The two young boys, formerly hellhounds, run alongside us.

"What if they won't take her, Myrtle?" Col asks.

"They'll take her," Myrtle says, sounding confident in this.

Shaken by events, I tremble violently, blood dripping from my lip, where my witchy mistress slapped me. I know nothing of this Grimm, whose men the young lad has been sent to talk to, but I'm already convinced he's the wickedest, most terrible creature. These people are about to hand me over to him for the promise of coins.

"But you know what Grimm's like," Col continues as we trek back to their farm. "Doesn't always pay. Sometimes he just takes it."

Myrtle huffs. "He won't take her from me. Even the fallen centaurs are wary of my kind. Grimm or one of his men will pay what is due, then take the lass and be on their way."

Her words offer no comfort. Moreover, they instill a greater sense of dread. What is this woman that would make the fallen centaur think twice before crossing her path? My thoughts shift to the two strange lads running alongside us in the forest, how they changed into hounds and back to human again. Are they sentient, I wonder, or something else entirely?

As the ramshackle farmstead comes into view at the end of the path, I worry about myself. Why didn't I speak to Calden? Why did I flee? I know him, the centaur whose bed I have shared every night since I arrived, and he is no cruel master. If I'd said I couldn't stay for the moon month, he might have let me go.

Only where would I go? This foolish flight was ill-conceived from the start. In my heart, I want to believe he will come for me, that he will rescue me like he rescued me from the raiders who sought to defile me. Only I have been ungrateful and have run, all because I do not think he loves me as I have come to love him.

There, I have admitted it, and that just makes me feel a thousand times worse.

As we reach the farm building, the two hounds are chained to either side of the front door. Here they sit in human form, staring out across the courtyard.

Inside, the home is worse than it appears from the outside. Dirt lingers everywhere, curtains little more than filthy rags, and stale rushes are upon the floor. Clutter covers every surface and most of the floor—books, scrolls, pots, jars, cloth wrapped bundles, barrels, and all manner of wooden widgets and assemblies. A sturdy wooden table is surrounded by a mismatch of chairs, one of which lies broken upon the floor.

My skin crawls when I see a rat scuttle across the hearth.

"Get a collar, Col," Myrtle says, taking hold of my arm.

"Is that a good idea?" Col asks. "It could render her insensible."

Collar? What is this collar? Is this what happened to the boys? Am I about to be turned into a horrible death hound and slave of this woman? I pull out of her hold and make a run for the door.

It slams shut before me, although neither Col nor Myrtle moved. Shuffling footsteps approach, even as my fingers grasp the handle and tug, but it does not open. How? How is this possible?

"Calm, lass," Col says. "We've sent word to the Grimm now, and there's no going back. Myrtle here has ways that the centaurs do not fool with, but they will surely be furious should they come here in hopes of taking an omega, only to find that she is gone."

I don't care about his problems, nor about suffering the wrath of these fallen centaurs, but I do care about myself and this burgeoning sense of horror. "Please, I won't tell anybody. Just let me leave." I continue to rattle the door handle furiously, hoping it might yield.

It does not, and as cruel fingers grasp my arms, the fight goes out of me. I tremble uncontrollably, gripped by my fear and this man, as Myrtle goes to a chest to the right of a cold stone fireplace. Thrusting aside tattered cloth sacks and worn books, she clears the top before working the latch. It opens with a creak, and she rummages inside before rising with a slim leather collar in her grasp.

"Please, no." I shake my head, trying to back up, but I have nowhere to go. The door is locked by an otherworldly power, and I am a prisoner of their home. Yet even this pales beside the prospect of this witch collaring me. Wickedness emanates from that seemingly innocuous strip of leather, one that leaves me cold with dread.

I whimper, seized by a terrible feeling that my life is over should she complete her task. I struggle and kick out, but the old man is strong and I cannot break free.

"Keep the lass steady," Myrtle says. She comes closer and closer, a sense of menace coming with her.

Fisting my hair, Col holds me as she snaps it shut around my throat.

Lethargy overcomes me, and I sink to my knees. There is no longer any need for them to subdue me. My limbs no longer follow my command. Inside, I am screaming. Outside, I am a voiceless shell.

"What shall we do with her?" Col asks.

"May as well put her to work," Myrtle says. "What is your name, lass?"

"Hope," I say under compulsion, barely above a whisper.

"Hope. Get to work. Clean the home."

I have no desire to obey her, yet I do so anyway. The lethargy recedes, and I rise like a sleepwalker, take a broom from beside the door, and begin to clear up the mess.

CHAPTER FOURTEEN

Hope

I toil all day, body moving from one task to another utterly against my will. I sweep, mop, dust, and set chaos to order, but inside, I am frantic, my mind whirling between past events and my future.

The farmstead door lies open. Col and Myrtle are both outside much of the day, but I have no means of escape without control over my body. As dusk falls, the young lad, Reggie, returns on the horse.

"What did they say?" Myrtle demands as the lad sits at the long bench and begins shoveling the stew I have cooked into his mouth. I have come to understand Myrtle is very much in charge here. Whatever unwholesome power she possesses raises her above both the men.

"Called me a liar," Reggie says around mouthfuls of food. "Said they would pass the news onto Grimm and he might be along later in the week."

Myrtle clicks her tongue. Col sends her a worried look. "Said this wasn't a good idea," he says. "Don't like those fallen centaurs sniffing around here."

"Quiet, Col," Myrtle says. "Let me handle this. Have I led us wrong before?"

"No," Col concedes.

When supper is over, Myrtle instructs Reggie, "Take the lass to the pen." A leash is attached to my collar, and I'm taken outside.

The pen turns out to be an open stable block, guarded by the two lads who are once more in their hellhound form. He attaches my leash to a ring in the wall, snags a rough blanket from a hook by the door, and tosses it at me. Hands on hips, he stares down at me.

"I've heard about you savage lasses," he says, gaze trailing over my exposed legs.

I snatch the blanket up and pull it over me, not liking how he leers.

"No need to be shy, lass. I heard your kind needs regular rutting."

I swallow past the dryness in my throat, understanding that I am at the mercy of this foul man.

He cups his cock through his pants. "Want a bit of this? You omegas are like a bitch in heat for the taste of a man's cock."

It's all I can do not to gag.

"Reggie!" Myrtle's shrill call is music to my ears. She stands on the front step of the house, glaring at her son. "Get indoors."

He winks at me and gives his cock another squeeze through his pants. "Got plenty to give you, lass."

"Reggie!" The next call is a brisk command, and he snaps to attention, swinging around and stomping for the house.

I let out a ragged breath as the door to the farmstead closes with a bang. The two hounds eyeball me before settling down on their haunches and closing their eyes.

I'm shaking, fearful and cold, my stomach is in knots, and I am exhausted yet certain I won't find rest. Swallowing thickly, I consider the collar around my throat. It seems straightforward that I might remove it, but the sickness rolling in my stomach every time my fingers stray toward it tells me it will not end well. I opt to touch the lead, that is all…but my body revolts. I'm on my hands and knees, muscles convulsing and sweat breaking out across my skin as I retch, bringing up a small amount of water and food.

The hounds rouse from sleep and watch me as I sit back against the wooden wall, a trembling mess. Do I need to be stronger? Could I find the will necessary to push past this? It is a simple task, to remove a buckled collar… I try again and again until I must accept that it is beyond me.

I collapse on my side, shaking uncontrollably, utterly wretched.

Somehow, I sleep.

I rise.

My life falls into a pattern. One day turns into two, turns to day three. I toil for Myrtle, and I sleep in the open stable with a meager blanket for warmth. My despair grows, as does Reggie's interest. He leers openly at me when his mother or father are not around.

As if the situation were not bad enough, my breasts are swollen and ache all the time. Worse, they begin to leak a clear sticky liquid that stains the front of my dress. Reggie can't stop looking at it.

It is the bitterest, most desperate feeling, for I wish that I was nestled in Calden's arms with his mouth upon me. I have no hunger, for he has broken me for anything but him. I dream about him, snatches of memories as I fitfully sleep, then wake up sobbing for I am cold and alone.

"She needs milking," Reggie says, stirring me from turning over the soil on the vegetable plot. At first, I wonder what he is talking about, given they only have two scrawny goats for milk and I saw to them this morning.

I swallow uneasily as I realize he is staring at my breasts.

Myrtle, who is standing nearby, clips him round the ear.

"Ow! Fuck!" he mutters under his breath.

"Don't fucking touch her," Myrtle says. "Grimm will be here soon enough, and he won't want her after your poxy cock has been inside her."

The old man chuckles, pausing his work repairing a fence.

"I'm only saying," Reggie says sullenly, shooting me a glare like it is my fault he has gotten into trouble.

I go back to my hoeing, Reggie's eyes following me. It's only a matter of time before he courts his mother's wrath and acts anyway. They say I'm an omega, but what does that mean? I can't believe it is true, but they seem certain of it.

Is this my fate?

What will happen if Grimm does not come?

What will happen if he does?

I worry, telling myself it is better or worse one way or the other. I pray to the Goddess every night that Calden might come for me.

He doesn't.

I have finished with the garden work and gathered a bucket and mop to clean the home when I hear the unmistakable sound of hooves. My heart flutters wildly within the cage of my ribs, and I turn in the direction of the forest path. I want so badly for it to be Calden. It feels as though my will alone might make it happen.

Fevered prayers are muttered under my breath. How good I will be, how grateful, how I will never run again!

From the first glimpse, I know it is not Calden nor any of his herd. The bucket and mop drop from my nerveless fingers, crashing to the floor, splattering water all over my ankles and the weed riddled cobbles. I take a step backward, gripped by mindless terror.

The fallen centaur.

There are three of them, and they are dressed for battle, with plate and leather armor upon both the beastly and human parts of their body. They do not carry spears, as Axton's herd does, but wicked-looking curved axes. The leader wears a helm adorned by a set of curved horns. He is a fearsome-looking individual, with a stunning chestnut coat, a braided blond beard, and pale eyes hidden within his helm. Muscular arms bunch as he shifts the ax and tucks it into a strap around his waist. He is the most formidable male I've ever seen. The urge to prostrate myself before him is strong, but I refuse to. Such deference is for Calden only.

Reggie slinks off, Col watches warily, but Myrtle steps forward boldly. In ragged clothes and with a nest of gray hair, this filthy woman smiles broadly like a queen before her subjects. "Grimm," she says, bowing gracefully.

The lead centaur removes his helm from his head, revealing long hair the same shade of golden brown as his tail. I want him to look as monstrous as I sense he is, but assuredly, he is a wicked kind of handsome, for all his eyes are cold. His attention shifts, not toward my mistress, but toward me. He trots a few steps closer, and his spicy scent flows over me, making my belly clench in a most unpleasant way. He surveys me from head to toe, gaze lingering upon my breasts. His nostrils flare, and he stomps his hooves against the broken cobbles. I must steel myself not to cower away.

"Ripe," he says, voice low and gravely. "What a fine prize you have found."

Myrtle bows her head magnanimously. "I knew you'd be pleased. As soon as I caught her sleeping in our barn, I sent for you. She says she's from Axton's herd."

Grimm's eyes narrow upon Myrtle. "Axton?" My mistress is still busy preening and does not notice the sudden restlessness within the three centaurs gathered. "Did you steal her?"

"I did not," Myrtle says, voice high with chagrin. "She was stowed away in our barn."

"Why does she have a collar around her neck?" he asks. "Did you place it there? Is it one of your sick toys? I do not wish for a witless woman."

"I have done nothing," Myrtle says. "She arrived on a horse. Mayhap she fled Axton's herd. Can't think of any other reason for her to be here."

"If you bring their wrath upon me, I will not be pleased."

"He has been nowhere near us in the past number of days. Likely he doesn't trouble himself with a lass fleeing when he has a pregnant mate. And she is not witless at all."

"Good," Grimm says decisively. "Take the collar off."

My eyes dart between them, and I swallow in anticipation of her removing the hideous collar. I wonder what Grimm will do. Does he fear Axton after all? Will he return me to them?

The centaur on his left edges forward to stand beside Grimm, his coat a liver dun, and his hair dark and wild, shaved into a mohawk. Like Grimm, his beard is similarly braided. "If she is witless, we should take her back to Axton just for the fun of it."

Grimm chuckles. "Aye, some compensation in the form of amusement at his expense. Imagine the look upon his face." His sharp gaze returns to Myrtle. "He would dispense swift justice upon the old hag for playing with one of his."

Myrtle laughs nervously. "I didn't play you, Grimm. The lass is sound of mind, and you do not fear Axton's reprisal for keeping her either way."

My burgeoning hope that this might see me returned to Axton is dashed when Grimm inclines his head. "I do not fear Axton, this is true, but I do not want a witless woman either. Come, take that wretched collar off so I might assess her for myself."

Myrtle steps toward me. I hate the thought of her hands upon me, but the relief as she unbuckles the collar and thrusts it toward Col is heartfelt. My hands go to my throat, closing over the flesh as the sick feeling dissipates and free will returns to my body and mind. I stand before the huge centaur, trembling. Now that the collar is gone, my limbs are frozen with fear.

"She is not running," the center beside Grimm says, indicating me.

The third centaur steps forward to join them. "Come, lass, speak if you can."

My mind spins through scenarios. Should I play witless? Grimm said he would take me back to Axton, for his amusement. My eyes shift warily between them. Can I do this? I think I can do anything if it might only see me taken home.

"Rut her, Barok," Grimm says, nodding toward me. "If she doesn't struggle, we'll know for sure."

I fight not to show a reaction that would give me away. The centaur to his left grins, tucks his ax into his belt, and trots toward me.

A squeal escapes my lips, and laughter follows me when I turn and run. The centaur chases me down with ease, picks me up, and tosses me over his shoulder. I scream and thrash, but he pins a strong arm around the back of my legs. "Not witless," he confirms cheerfully.

"So it would appear," Grimm agrees. "It was a good ruse to find out for sure. We will take her."

Despair comes for me. I curse myself as much as them. If only I could have controlled myself. Likely they wouldn't even have rutted me, for they seem to relish my spirit. I beat upon the monster's back, kick and flail. It does me no good. He is strong, and all my fighting does cause their collective laughter to rise.

"The coin," Myrtle calls out.

The centaur carrying me stills. Through the curtain of my hair, I peer back.

The witchy woman stalks over to Grimm, expecting her due.

"You think I'll give you coin?" Grimm says. "I do not fear Axton, but nor do I court his interference. You will speak of this to no one, certainly not to Axton. I do not wish him or his righteous herd snooping around my lands. If he comes here, tell him you have never seen the lass, and be sure he's convinced. If any of this comes back to me, rest assured, I will burn your shitty little farm to the ground…and you at the stake. Do not expect coins for your meddling. You will get no reward from me."

Myrtle screeches.

Grimm turns, intent upon riding out.

"Release the hounds!"

Reggie is at the stable, where the two lads are leashed to posts.

With a slash of his hand, the two lads transform into hellhounds. Another scream tears from my lips as the beasts bound straight toward us. Grimm is quicker. The ax swings, cleaving through the nearest hound as it leaps for him.

Its howl is horrifying as it collapses to the floor in a bloody, broken heap. The third centaur closes in on the other side and strikes the head clean off the second hound.

"No!" Myrtle wails, throwing herself at the dead hounds. "My babies," she cries, sobbing as she hugs the hideous hound to her breast.

Grimm snorts and tucks his ax back into the hook at his waist. "I have not killed your babies," Grimm says coldly. "You killed them yourself many moons ago." Turning to his centaurs, Grimm says, "We ride."

CHAPTER FIFTEEN

Hope

With the binding on my wrists secured around the mohawked centaur's waist, I ride upon his back through the forest, across streams, and through villages and hamlets.

The forest pathway rises steeply, and a vast fortress rises into the clouds before us. Drab gray walls present an austere façade that instills a sense of foreboding in me. The centaurs on duty wear the same battle garb, and rather than the cherry greeting I came to associate with Axton's herd, they merely nod to their leader.

"Has the patrol returned?" Grimm asks them.

"Yes, Grimm," the centaur on duty says. "More spiders come through. It was bloody and some were seriously injured. They are being tended by our healers." His eyes skitter from Grimm to me, and his nostrils flare. "A chosen one?"

Grimm nods, glancing back at me. "She was from Axton's herd. Fled them, according to the witch. I'll call a meeting this evening."

The two centaurs on sentry bow their heads in deference, and Grimm trots forward. Barok follows behind. The pathway is steep, and soon, we rise higher than the tops of the forest canopy, where a sharp wind buffets us. The ground turns rocky to either side of the path and falls steeply off. Ahead looms an entrance of monumental proportions.

The magnitude of my situation settles upon me like a heavy weight, for it would be near impossible to penetrate such a fortress and equally hard to flee. Were there no straps around my wrist, and were Barok not holding them, I might consider a simpler fate of falling to my death. I'm not one for being fatalistic, yet every step along the steep path, every clack of hooves, is a step away from Calden.

That brief time with him is all but a distant dream. My time with Myrtle and while I wore the collar scoured many sweet memories away. I sense events within this imposing fortress will purge me of all those remaining. I am sorrowful beyond measure, but my eyes remain dry. Inside, I weep, filled by cold, bitter desperation that forces me to acknowledge this situation is of my own making. Despite this, resolve strengthens within me. No, I shall not dash to my death, and neither shall this be the last place I see.

More guards stand before the soaring entrance. They nod to Grimm and throw open the two heavy wooden doors. We trot through into a grand stone hall with tall support columns reaching a high vaulted ceiling. Braziers are lit, their flames dancing and casting shadows against the columns lining the central path. To left and right, high windows cast weak light onto the flagstones before us, the centaur hooves clattering as we pass through. Centaurs and humans move through the space with purpose, while others peer down at us from a balcony on either side.

To the front, a raised dais holds a fur covered throne-like structure that could only be for a centaur.

"Take her to the stable," Grimm says. "Ensure she is prepared."

Barok nods and turns left, entering into a long stone corridor with flickering sconces upon walls as high and wide as necessary to accommodate a centaur. The fortress inhabitants turn to watch me as we pass. A myriad of emotions is evidenced upon their faces— curiosity, appraisal, and pity.

Barok trots through another huge wooden door. On the other side, I am surprised to find a courtyard. The fortress does not sit in isolation among the clouds as I first thought, but rather, backs onto a plateau. Behind the high stone walls and battlements surrounding the courtyard peeps the canopy of a forest. Directly opposite the fortress, embedded in the outer wall, is a set of substantial wooden double gates.

A strange blue glow emanates from that direction.

"What is that?" I ask.

"The portal," Barok says, cutting right across the courtyard.

I stare after the glow. *A portal?* I have only heard about them in tales. It's said they lead to other worlds, where strange ungodly creatures roam. I shudder. Is this the source of the spiders the guard mentioned when we arrived? Why do I have a terrible feeling that they are not the good kind of spider that sits in the corner of the ceiling and keeps the other pests at bay?

A great bellow goes up. A horn sounds.

My head swings in the direction of the commotion, fear gripping me as men and centaurs rush to the battlements.

"What's happening? Are we under attack?"

"We are always under attack," Barok says calmly, paying no heed to the sounding horn and cries that call to arms. Trotting around the side of the fortress, he approaches a stable block.

I expect horses.

There are no horses.

Rows of stalls line a central passage. Where horse stalls would be open, these are closed off by sturdy lattice metal doors. Inside, upon straw beds, are human women with collars around their throats. They sit huddled in the corners, most naked, but some partially covered by threadbare blankets.

But it is not pity for the subjugated women that captures my attention. At the far end is an open space, and under the flickering light of sconces, is a wooden assembly. A woman is strapped down against a saddle, one all too familiar to me. Her breasts hang down to either side, and reins have been attached to her nipples, held in the hands of a giant black centaur mounting her. As he flicks the reins, her breast jiggle, driving a wilder moan from her lips, one I cannot readily say is pleasure or pain.

My body contracts as fear and humiliation for her sends a shiver rippling down my spine. The power as the great centaur ruts her tiny body is absolute. The heavy sacks of his furred balls sway with every thrust as his monstrous cock plows her vulnerable pussy. I am horrified and ashamed to find my breath quickening and my breasts aching anew.

She is defenseless before him, utterly subjugated, and yet I cannot fully shake the feeling that she also takes pleasure from what he does.

Her cries latch upon sensitive nerves under my skin. The rich scent of centaur musk is prevalent in the air, filling my nose and lungs. Beyond the open stable door comes the sound of the horn and the cries of centaurs and humans at war.

It is debauched, depraved, and unsettling in every way.

I begin to fret as my captor stops before an empty stall. He untethers my wrists and plucks me from his back before depositing me on the clean stall floor.

"I'll be back later," he says, lips tugging up in a grin. His fierce face and wild mohawk casts him into an otherworldly light. The lattice door to my prison is swung shut with a rattle, and a rusty padlock snapped into place.

I rise unsteadily as he steps back. "Got a new one, Clegg," he calls out. "Needs some food and water."

The fevered moans of the saddled woman reach a crescendo as a human man comes to join Barak before my stable door. Clegg has thick arms and a bald pate, and is decorated upon every bit of exposed flesh with fearsome tattoos. While his head may be bald, his long beard is braided in the same manner as the centaurs. He looks me up and down and sniffs. "I'll see to it," he says.

The woman being mounted lets out a piercing shriek in competition with the shouts and clattering hooves that emanate from the courtyard.

"I'll be back later, little pet," Barok says to me before he turns and trots out of the stable.

The tattooed overseer plants hands on hips and eyeballs me until the sound of approaching hooves draws his attention. The enormous black centaur trots past, nodding to the overseer.

"I'll be back," the overseer says to me before he disappears from view to tend to the mounted woman. He returns soon after, carrying her limp body, placing her against clean straw in the stall opposite me.

The woman is lovely, with long golden hair and pale, freckled skin. Then I see how slick and cum drips from her to the floor, how her nipples are engorged and pink, how the flesh of her ass is striped with welts. She moans softly as he settles a rough blanket over her, seeming to fall straight into a doze.

Goddess, what has been done to her?

Slamming her door shut, Clegg turns toward me.

Is this my new fate?

I believe that it is.

As he unlocks my gate, my body and mind shift toward fight-or-

116

flight.

I cannot be here. I cannot stay here. I cannot be reduced to a mindless receptacle for these dreaded centaurs' seed.

The overseer reads me with ease. Taking me by the arm, he snatches up a crop hanging from the wall outside the stall and lands a series of savage blows upon my ass and thighs.

I squeal and thrash.

It does me no good.

I am marched out along the corridor, into the back, and past the hideous assembly that stirs my curiosity, even as it makes me shudder. Beyond the mounting room is a row of rainwater showers. I am stripped. The crop lashes me whenever I fight his commands. Naked, I am thrust under the spout and ordered to clean.

He pulls a chain, and water rains down over me. It is ice cold, and I shiver as I scrub myself down, weeping with pity as the crop stings my vulnerable flesh to keep me in check. When I am done to his satisfaction, I am hauled from the room, still dripping, back through the stable and thrust into my stall. A bucket of water is poured into a trough I only now notice on one side of the stall. Beside it is another trough, where a ladleful of sloppy mash is dumped.

"Eat," the overseer instructs before slamming my cell shut and heaving the heavy chain into place. "Looks like Barok wants you for himself. He uses the stable frequently, but I heard he was looking for a mate." His grin is cruel. "Even the well-broken lasses used to saddling weep when he's done with 'em. He usually spreads his attention around. Got our work cut out, stretching your cunt out so he won't tear you the first time. You'll get used to it. They all do. And if you don't, well, there are spiders on the other side of the wall that enjoy rutting the ones as can't satisfy the centaurs, and we'll toss you over there. Be a good lass and accept our orders, and it'll go easier on you."

Warning issued, he pivots and stalks off.

I reach the corner where the straw is deepest before my legs give out. All the tears I have held back fall in great, gut-wrenching sobs.

Outside the stable, the roar of battle has faded. The horn no longer blares, and the only sounds are those of my endless sorrow.

When I can rouse myself, it is to find the pretty lass opposite peering at me through the lattice of the door. "We all cry at first," she says. "I promise, you will come to accept it. Don't mind what he says about the spiders. There's not a centaur nor man here as won't fight to the death to save us from their kind. Soon, we all realize there are worse things than a lusty centaur, and they all live on the other side of the wall."

CHAPTER SIXTEEN

Calden

With every day that passes, the sickness roiling within me grows. My mind and body succumb to a kind of fever. I cannot sleep, my awareness is heightened, and my focus is razor-sharp.

On the fifth day, we come upon the farmstead. One look, and a sickly awareness worms in my gut.

"I don't like this," Gael says as he trots beside me.

The air holds an unnatural stillness disturbed only by the clatter of our hooves against the weed riddled courtyard. Among the weeds, I note a dark stain that immediately brings to mind blood. It has an abandoned feeling, although the weary plume of smoke rising from the farmstead chimney suggests otherwise.

"Magic," Gael says.

I nod slowly. The farmstead door swings open, and a wild-looking woman emerges, gray of hair, stout of posture. She recoils on seeing us. "Be gone, foul heathens."

I share a look with Gael. "We are not the heathens," Gael says as we trot forward.

The woman makes a sign upon her chest. Not the sign of the Goddess, but some kind of devilish symbol that sets the hairs prickling upon the back of my neck.

An elderly man emerges from the barn to our left, fingers curling with nervous agitation around his pitchfork's handle, joined by a younger lad who is equally twitchy.

Everything about this place makes me uneasy.

"She has been here," I say. A statement, not a question.

"Nobody has been here," the stout woman says. "Go about your business. We don't want your kind around."

For good measure, she spits upon the ground.

I slam the butt of my spear against the cobbles, and the woman recoils.

Hope has been here. "Your magic does not work on centaurs, witch. What have you done with my mate?"

"Mate?" She is thoroughly flustered now, and I step forward, leveling the spear upon her. She trembles, although she tries to hold her ground. I recognize guilt when I see it.

"What has happened here? Where is she?" I come to a stop before her, my spear tip leveled upon her throat. The thought of Hope being here, of her even crossing paths with this ungodly woman, escalates my rage.

An unnatural force stops me from pressing further forward. Although the witch does not move, sweat breaks out upon her brow. My arm begins to ache with the pressure, and I shift it back a fraction, although I do not move it away. "Where. Is. She?" I repeat.

Gael steps to my left, placing himself to better watch the two men, lest they take foolish action as my mind sinks into a frenzy.

"I know nothing about your mate. The only centaurs as pass through here are the dark kind, and I want nothing to do with them either."

"What have you done?" I ask.

She shakes her head and tries to step back. Although my spear cannot touch her, I slam it into the doorframe beside her, blocking her retreat.

"Myrtle," the older man calls.

"Shut up, Col," she hisses.

"Reckon we should string these two up," Gael says. "To help loosen up her tongue."

"The lass was nothing but a fucking nuisance," the lad says. "Got my brothers killed."

"Reggie, shut your mouth," the old woman screeches.

I shift to the side, blocking her view of the two men.

"Reggie," I say. "You seem like a reasonable lad who doesn't want to die today. My mate has been taken. I suggest you learn to loosen your tongue lest you want to follow your brothers into the ground."

Around me, I detect the faintest tendril of the fallen centaurs. *Grimm*. The dreadful sensation in my chest grows. My heart's desire is not here. "Tell me what unfolded," I say, enunciating each word.

"She slept in the barn," the lad says. "We found her the next morning. She tried to run, but we—"

"Reggie," the woman snarls.

"They took her," the lad continues in a rush.

"When?" I demand, never taking my eyes from the witch. Her magic may not work upon us, but her kind possess many tricks.

"Yesterday," the old man says.

My nostrils flare, and my hand shakes upon the handle of my spear. I yank it back.

"Tell me you were kind to her. Tell me you treated her well."

The woman shakes her head. "I'd never hurt the lass. Can't you see I'm grieving," she says. "You have no business here."

She is lying. "Did you treat her well?!"

"Stupid omega," the woman says, spittle flying from my mouth. "Caused nothing but trouble."

"We never harmed her," the old man calls. "But we sent for Grimm. He pays well for her kind. Only he didn't pay and took her anyway. Grimm and two of his lieutenants have taken her back to the fortress at Dires End."

"You think the fallen centaurs are the only ones to fear? Burn the fucking house down, Gael," I say. "Burn it all."

We leave the burning farmstead where an old witch weeps and curses us. Finally, I know where my heart is, but now that I do, I wish she were anywhere else.

Gael is silent as we ride to rendezvous with Axton and the herd. My body is coiled with tension. I want to ride now, to charge Dires End where they hold her, but I have no fucking chance on my own.

The fallen centaur. I am aware of what they do to sweet young women like Hope—the training, the stable, where centaurs slake their lust and leave their sweet charges alone of a night among straw like they are animals instead of cuddling them and keeping them warm.

I called her my mate, but the truth is, she is not. Grimm is not well known for his compassion. Most likely, he will fucking laugh and tell me to be on my way, lest his centaurs run us all through should we seek to claim her back. I will not fucking go, not without her. I will slay every fucking centaur and man until I have her safe where she belongs.

A moon month? That is over now. She will find herself in a new debt, and the length of her servitude to me will be indefinite.

If I get her back, the little voice in my head taunts, but I cannot think about that now. She was mine to care for and protect. I saved her from ruffians, not that she might find herself in this fate. She stowed away in their barn, took a horse and ran. *Why?* I thought we were growing to love one another. I thought she cared for me as I had come to care for her. She fucking fed from me…and then she ran.

Her plump ass will be sore after I welt it good, lest she be confused about leaving a centaur she swore a sacred debt to.

As agreed, we meet on the edge of a gorge with the other hunters of the valley who have been searching for my wayward, soon-to-be mate. Axton is talking to Brin, but he looks up, seeing my approach.

"We have found her," I say. "Taken by Grimm."

Collective murmurs go up among those assembled. Axton trots over to me. "When?"

"Yesterday, sold out to him, from reading between the lines, by the old witch down at Tinder lane."

He nods before cutting a look to his left. "Brin, Aiden, get my battle gear. Meet us at Piper crossing."

"I cannot let you challenge him," I say. Axton's nostrils flare as he turns back to me. "You have a mate and a herd to consider. If there is war, that is different, but if there is a challenge, that is mine and mine alone."

His eyes are full of fire. He is the more powerful male. He is the herd leader, and he has ever assumed that role with vigor and honor. If it came down to it, he would have a better chance than me, but his heart is not on the line in this matter, mine is.

"The Goddess set Hope on my path, and I believe that if she belongs there, with me, she will surely guide my hand again."

He nods to Brin and Aiden. "Get the battle gear. It might not be me wearing it, but we will have need of it all the same." He turns back to me. "Grimm is a tricky bastard who does much for his sick amusement as for common sense. It is a hard life. They live so close to the portal, and mayhap the unholy things that spill out have addled their minds, even as they sharpen their battle skills. I cannot readily say if he would accept a challenge, but Hope is one of ours now and we are set upon a course. If it comes to a challenge, if he accepts it, then it is your right to meet it."

My chest rises, relief crashing through me, for I know this must be so.

"But only if that challenge is not with Grimm," Axton continues, never taking his eyes from mine and setting a cold sinking feeling in my gut. "No power of the Goddess will make you his match, and I would be no leader to stand back and watch you die. What will come to pass will be decided once we are there, and only then."

I nod, accepting, for I have no choice.

"Good," he says, now addressing the crowd of centaurs. "They have taken a moon debt. They have dared to claim one of ours. We cannot tolerate such an act, for we are a herd. All are equal before the Goddess, and all are equal within the herd."

A roar goes up, and spear butts thump against the ground. I roar with them and thump my spear with all the pent-up rage that I feel. A fire lights within me, one that demands an outlet.

"We ride for Dires End!" Axton calls. He leads the way, setting a fast pace that soothes my need for swift action.

We follow, riding throughout the day, meeting Brin and Aiden at the crossroads. As the sun sets, I sense that we are being followed by wolves who do Grimm's bidding. He will know we are coming.

He will also know why.

CHAPTER SEVENTEEN

Hope

I am roused three times during the night by the sound of the horn. The other women in the stable pay it no heed, but I am frantic with every repetition of that eerie battle sound.

I can't stop weeping. It's like the dam has opened and I cannot hold it back. I sleep very little, and I worry a lot. As dawn finally breaks, the burly overseer arrives, tossing food and water into the trough. My stomach is empty, but I have no appetite. I wish I were with Calden on his decadently soft bed, nestled in his arms. Instead, my foolishness has left me on a bed of itchy straw. My breasts are achy and swollen and leak the strange clear liquid all over my belly. Calden said the Goddess was changing me, but now I think I am not changing, but broken, and the fallen centaur will soon use me for their pleasure.

The pretty doe-eyed lass who rests in the opposite stall, who was rutted yesterday by the black centaur, is named Summer. Whenever I begin to fret, she sings softly for me in the most beautiful voice

I've ever heard. The tune is unknown to me, and the words are in another language, but it comforts me some.

Dawn breaks, bringing light to the stable and rousing me from a troubled doze. My eyes are puffy from my tears, and I'm wretched in every way. I wonder about escape, even though we are well secured.

Training. Yesterday, the overseer said that I needed training to take a centaur's cock. I shudder with revulsion until I think about Calden. His cock might be monstrous, yet I feel a tingling awareness just thinking about it.

I ache between my thighs, a distracting sensation. It is this place, for it stinks of centaur musk, and it has not escaped my notice that the rough blankets they gave me are likewise saturated. I hate it near me, but I'm chilled to the bone. I want to cling to the memory of Calden, what it felt like to be with him, and his scent. Still, he is not here, and the little I have seen of this great fortress suggests it is as hard to leave as it would be to penetrate in attack.

Likely, Calden has given up on me and instead taken pleasure from a sweet centaur female who can better slake his lusts and does not cause half the trouble I do.

I have been a poor moon debt to him, I realize. Now, he is like a distant dream. The passage of only a few weeks separates me from overhearing that conversation between Karl and Fiona. Then came the raiders and Calden. I experienced a taste of heaven upon earth before I was flung back into wretchedness again, for surely such joy is not for me.

"You need to eat some food," Summer says softly, leaning against the lattice of her stall door, watching me with worried eyes. "It won't harm you." Leaning forward, she dips a hand into the trough and sips water.

"They feed us like animals," I say, barely able to contain my revulsion at eating from the floor.

"We are pets to them," she says. "Better to accept that. I know you are new here, that you wish to fight, to resist, and perhaps harbor plans of escape." Her face softens. "They will not serve you well. I know these are not words you want to hear now. You want to know that there is some possibility. How did they come to find you?"

"I ran away," I say. "First from my human husband, and then from a proud centaur who is from a different Goddess worshiping tribe."

She gasps. "That is quite a tale. Why did you run from your husband?"

"He had a mistress, and they...well, *she* wanted to poison me so she might keep my home and things."

"What a witch!" she hisses in outrage.

My lips tug up. "Aye, she was, but not a real witch, for I met one of those later."

She leans in close to the metal lattice now, her attention rapt. "Is this with the other centaur? Was it when you fled? Are they wicked like the ones here? How did you get away?"

I shake my head. "No, they are not wicked. They were kind to me." I swallow, thinking of how I came to love him so swiftly...and how I was nothing to him. "When I fled my husband, raiders found me. Calden saved me and said I was his for a moon month, indebted to him. At the end of the month, he would have tossed me out anyway. I decided to leave early."

Her eyes narrow. "He is not such a nice centaur then. Saving a lass, only to cast her out. What kind of monster would do that? Mayhap he is worse than the centaurs here. I don't think he's decent at all. No wonder you ran. None of the centaurs here would let a lass leave."

"I wish they would," I say with meaning. "I am terrified of being saddled."

She chuckles. "It is not so bad. Quite the contrary, for the pleasure is intense, indescribable even. Their scent acts upon us, even betas, though the training is not pleasant, I'll give you that."

She quiets as one of the overseers walks past, rousing the woman sleeping in the stall next to Summer. The young woman squeaks a token protest, but he takes the crop from the nearby hook and swats her ass.

Her sharp squeal makes me start, but she quickly does his bidding. "It is Pearl's turn first today, it would seem," Summer says conversationally. "They use us frequently, for it aids their healing. There are several stables and several mounting benches in each. After battle or on return from patrol, they might be wounded and depleted, and the rutting revives them so they can fight again." She shrugs. "The Goddess is mysterious. When the fighting is fierce, they return here often and we must offer them what we can."

I turn toward the open doorway, where I can glimpse the sunshine. "Do they keep us here the whole time?" I ask, trying not to think about the creaking sounds and faint murmurs coming from the far end of the stable, where the mounting platform is.

"We are allowed out," she says. "Mostly, they keep us here when there are frequent attacks, so we are ready. It's a little cold at night, but not so bad. I was a slave of orcs before, which was not a good life. Here, I have food in my belly, and even so, I do not mind the centaurs. Sometimes I wish…" She trails off, distracted as we both are, when a great rattling sound comes from the direction of the courtyard. "One of the night patrols is returning."

"Wish what?" I ask, intrigued by the conversation.

"That one might claim me as a mate." She shrugs. "It sometimes happens if a lass is lucky." When I shake my head, she adds with a rueful smile, "Better one centaur than many."

We fall silent as a centaur with golden hair and pale coat trots down the passage between us. He is filthy and bears a laceration to his right hip, deep enough that he leaves a trail of blood.

"Lance is a fearsome warrior and a dark lover," she says, turning to follow his passage. "He will rut Pearl well."

Clegg stalks past again, going about duties elsewhere. Hearing the clatter of hooves, my stomach turns over, realizing that it is the sound of Lance's hooves hitting the trough. A low feminine moan is followed by a deeper, masculine growl and a loud slap.

I blink. Summer giggles. "He is only warming up her ass, stoking her arousal before he fills her." More sharp slaps follow, and her moans increase. I cannot see from here, thank the Goddess, but the sounds do unwelcome things to me. My pussy begins to throb, and my aching breasts grow uncomfortable.

The slapping stops, the silence broken by another low, elongated moan. "Good lass," I hear the centaur rumble. "You are needy today. Let me fill you all up."

The lass moans louder as his hooves clatter and the assembly begins to creak. Goddess help us. He is rutting her. I poke my fingers in my ears like that might block out the sounds.

Summer grins at me and shakes her head. "You cannot block such a lusty centaur out. Lance is wounded, but even so, he is rarely quick about it."

The thumping, his growls, the creaking, her moans, and the occasional thud creates a filthy symphony. He instructs her on how well she pleases him, how her pretty tits sway, how beautiful she looks saddled, and how he will fill her and reward her.

The thumping picks up in pace.

I cannot see them, yet I'm near insensible, skin flushed and body responding, even as I try to shut the wanton act out. What is wrong with me? Summer is correct. How can we remain detached? I do not want a strange centaur to fill me with his cock, nor do I desire whatever hideous training might occur as they prepare me to take such a huge male. Yet my traitorous mind skitters toward imagining how I might look saddled before Calden. My pussy aches, bringing an unwelcome sense of openness, while clear stickiness leaks from my breasts. I am utterly wretched as, beyond my view, a lass is rutted by a centaur and filled with his cock.

I go to the corner of my stall and curl up into a ball. It doesn't help, for the stable echoes with her wild pleasure and his lusty enjoyment.

My imagination carries me away. It is no longer Pearl but me who is saddled. Only it is not the large, hideous assembly here, but the more refined style I recall seeing in Lila's home. Oh, how I wish Calden had one. I would let him coax me and show me how I might adapt and be trained to take him. It is clear now that such things are possible and do not even damage a lass that I can tell. Certainly, Summer bears no lingering ill effects.

I realize that I might even scream with pleasure, as the saddled lass now does.

A single, long, drawn-out cry accompanies a cease to the wild thudding. "Good pet," the centaur croons. "My sweet, good little pet. How well you have pleased me. How well you have taken my gift."

These gentle, if filthy words are not those of a cruel monster who only takes. Clearly, he has likewise given the lass pleasure in return.

But my heart does not belong to this centaur, nor any of the others here, for it has already been claimed and I could not abide another's touch. The overseer, Clegg, is summoned, and Lance trots past to exit the stable.

So begins my day. He is not the first nor the last, but one of an endless parade of centaurs. Young women are selected and taken from stalls, placed upon the mounting block, and rutted. They are carried back to their stalls, limp and insensible, dripping cum, sometimes still moaning and twitching as they come down from the high. The longer the day goes on, the more I dread the moment when my training might begin, for I know soon that it will be my turn.

It is not the overseer who comes for me, but Barok with a stoic expression that brings a quiver to my lips and coldness to my belly. He unlocks my door with a scowl on his face.

"You are not for the stable," he says. "Grimm has given his permission for me to take you as a mate."

I gasp as the lattice door swings wide open with a creak. Barok trots in, snatching me up from where I cower in the corner, and tosses me over his shoulder. My hair covers me in a curtain, and I push it away, sending a frantic glance toward Summer.

"Good luck." She waves, a bright smile upon her face...one I do not return.

I don't know whether it is worse to be claimed as a centaur's mate or used by many. Logic and Summer's earlier words tell me that it is better to belong to one, but I don't think my heart can take it, nor my soul, which shrivels up inside me. I thrash and struggle, determined not to go easily. I wonder if he is taking me to his private room, quarters, stable, or whatever residence he might have. Instead, he enters the fortress, hooves ringing against the flagstones until he comes out into the vast hall with soaring columns once again. Here, I find an assembly. I twist this way and that, trying to peer through the curtain of my hair. A crowd of centaurs and humans has gathered.

The world tumbles as I am dropped before the raised dais and throne. Dire wolves sit to either side, while Grimm lies sprawled upon his fur covered throne. Two human women, beautiful and naked, nestle before him. He plays with the hair of one, as the other rests her head against his flank.

I heave a breath, my focus shifting to the dire wolves. "A challenge then," Grimm says as he unfolds himself, and the two women move aside as he rises and takes the three steps until he is standing before me.

Challenge?

Something tickles my nose, a strange, familiar scent that leads to a prickling awareness. I follow Grimm's line of sight.

My chest heaves unsteadily, and I swear my whole body sways toward *him*. Calden, but not the Calden that I know. No, this version is monstrous, adorned in battle garb much like the centaurs here, in leather and metal, with spikes and plates that cover both the beastly and the human parts of him. A helm rests on his head topped with two huge curving horns, while in his hand is not his usual spear, but a great war sword that must be easily my height. I blink, trying to take this in, trying to assimilate this warrior with the sweet centaur I once knew. I see none of that. The new Calden is cold and terrifying, yet I love him so much, it is like a thread pulling me toward him, demanding that I *go*.

I gather myself, set to scramble for his arm, when a rattling growl brings me up short. Before me is a great furred monster—a dire wolf. With teeth curled, he dares me to move. Another stalks forward, cutting my path off, positioning around me where they lie, watching me, keeping me in place. I take a faltering step back, noticing the dozen centaurs who stand with Calden.

My love does not come alone, for his herd is here with him.

"I accept the challenge," Calden calls out. "You took what was mine."

I shake, feeling the potency of those words, locking my knees so I remain upon my feet. How I want to be his, forever, and not just for now, yet I am nothing more than an obligation and a debt to him, one that has caused him no end of trouble from beginning to end. Oh, why did he come here? Why does he make me hope? Does he have feelings for me? But no, he can't.

Challenge? He said a challenge, but who is he going to challenge? Does he challenge Grimm?

"Goddess," I murmur weakly. The thought of Calden's beautiful body suffering to defend me after my own foolishness is more than I can stand.

"No," I cry out. "You can't do this."

Calden's eyes do not move toward me, for he is staring straight at Grimm.

"She has been claimed," Grimm says, amused by my outburst. As he indicates the centaur who brought me here, and I recall Barok's earlier declaration that he would mate me. "She used to belong to you, now she belongs to Barok, who will claim her as his mate."

"Then I challenge Barok," Calden says coolly.

In the heated frenzy of my mind, I reason that Barok is not much less of a threat than Grimm. "I beg you, do not do this."

"I will not leave you here," Calden says, finally lowering his eyes to me. I see his determination there and his sense of responsibility for me. Surely he is the noblest of beings to willingly accept battle and possibly mortal injury that he might rescue me.

I cannot allow that. I could not bear it. "I do not want you to," I lie. "I do not want you to challenge." The words tumble out, anything I can think of that might stop this madness. How they wound, how I see the pain hardening his jaw, how I must steel myself not to throw myself before him and beg for forgiveness.

A tic thumps in his jaw, and his nostrils flare, fire charging his beautiful eyes. "That is not your choice." He turns away from me, looking now toward Barok. "The challenge stands."

No, this cannot happen. I dare to step forward, but the snap of the nearest dire wolf's jaws sees me stumble back. I sink to my knees, shaking uncontrollably. No, he cannot mean to fight. He cannot!

Barok laughs. "It would seem the lass has chosen. Looks like I will be the one breeding her, not you, Calden."

Calden's jaw locks as the taunt settles in. "Take up your armor, heathen," Calden snarls. "Or I will fight you as you are."

133

Human men hasten forward, swift to assemble the battle gear upon Barok. All the while, I am trapped before the dais, surrounded by dire wolves who will not let me pass. Grimm returns to his throne, settling down as if ready for a show. His two human pets return to his side, stroking him, and he shares a kiss with one, then the other, like a battle is not about to commence.

I tear my gaze away, lost in a spell that casts a shadow of surrealism over the situation. Armor fitted, Barok takes up his ax. My heart rate pounds heavily in my throat as the crowd parts and recedes into the shadow, giving the two warriors space.

Axton steps forward, speaking quietly to Calden before joining the rest of his herd members.

The floor before the dais is empty, save the two warriors who will fight over me. I sob piteously, feeling as though I'm caught in the grip of the most dreadful nightmare, one that I cannot escape. The tension is palpable as the two centaurs circle one another. They are equal in size and height, yet I'm terrified for Calden and would do anything that he might not suffer a single scratch.

These fallen centaurs are nothing like Axton's herd. They are battle hardened and live at constant war with the monsters from the portal. Still, I must consider the way Calden dispensed with the raiders who sought to harm me, of his battle with the bear shifter, and the many scars that already litter his beautiful coat. I understand that he, too, is no stranger to conflict.

They circle, hooves clacking on the flagstones. Barok swings his ax like he tests the weight before gripping it in both hands. Calden's sword is monstrous and must likewise be held in two hands.

The tension rises, like a war drum in my blood…and then they both charge, powerful hind legs kicking off as their weapons clash with a mighty clang. The crowd roars. They break away, only to meet once again. Sparks fly as the sharpened edges slide together, powerful legs bunching and quivering as they push against one another.

The immense power in their bodies is realized as they duel with one another. It is undoubtedly the most terrifying sight when two centaurs battle.

They are otherworldly in their prowess.

They were meant to battle monsters, not each other, yet they do, both wanting me.

Calden said I was his, yet I still do not know what that means and am terrified to hope. Barok's curving ax catches Calden's flank, and red blood spills down his beautiful, dappled coat. I wish I could take the blow, for I would gladly give my life to keep him safe. That is not my choice, for the Goddess has determined that these two males must fight.

The crowd cheers and jeers. Calden is the interloper here, the stranger. He does not have the backing of most, who chant their approval for Barok. Still, Calden has his herd with him, and they call their encouragement too, as the warriors circle, slash, clash weapons, and trade blows with fists or hooves. They rear, front hooves clattering against armor. Calden swings around, kicking his hind legs, and sending Barok flying back.

Barok shakes his head and springs back, battle ax swinging and landing with brutal force against the plate armor around Calden's beastly ribs. Calden parries, his sword swinging to find an opening at Barok's shoulder, cutting into flesh.

They battle on, clashing over and over. The wounds come on both sides. Calden is limping, but Barok holds his left arm awkwardly around his waist.

I cannot look, yet I cannot look away, weeping silent tears and praying that the owner of my heart might live.

Then the battle becomes a frenzy. Calden thrusts the tip of his sword between plated armor into Barok's side. Silence falls. The blade is yanked free, and Calden pivots and kicks, sending his opponent flying across the flagstone and crashing into a stone pillar. A brazier overturns, and hot coals spill over the flagstones, sending smoke curling up toward the high vaulted ceilings.

Barok's hooves clatter as he tries to rise, blood gushing from the wound. Calden is on him, knocking the ax away from his grasp, sending it skittering across flagstones to join the overturned brazier.

"Yield!" Calden says, his chest heaving and sword leveled upon Barok's throat. "Yield, or I will end you."

Barok roars, his hooves clattering again as he seeks to gain his feet.

"Yield!" Calden roars.

Barok's chest rises on unsteady breaths, his beastly body judders, and more blood pools out. "I yield."

Silence settles over the area. Nobody moves to aid the fallen centaur, but nor do they attack.

"A fair challenge," Grimm announces. He snaps his fingers, and the dire wolves rise and trot over to join their master. "Go, take the human, and do not come here again unless you seek war."

Axton steps forward to stand beside Calden. "Do not take what is ours again," Axton says, his voice carrying across the hall. "Unless *you* wish for war."

Grimm throws his head back and laughs. "You make a fair point. Take her, and let us tend to our fallen one. Unlike your paltry quarrels, our fight to survive does not stop for a challenge. When you are ready to play your part against the monsters of the void instead of hiding in your pretty valley, playing at war with bear shifters, then you may coach me on matters of war. Until then, take better care of your charges."

Trotting forward, Calden takes me up into his arms, where I weep, and without hesitation, throw my arms around his neck.

CHAPTER EIGHTEEN

Hope

Leaving the fortress, we enter the forest. As we travel, I worry for Calden and the terrible injuries that have been done to him.

Soon, we reach a river, and here I am put down and given leave to wash. Several herd members gather around Calden and help him remove the battle gear. I go about my business in the shallows of the river, but all I can think about is the way his beautiful body weeps blood. That is my fault. I did this to him, running away like a fool. Tears of sorrow and shame spill down my cheeks.

I am naked, but my state of undress hardly troubles me anymore. Bending, I scoop up water, sip a little, then wash my hands and face before tackling the stickiness that weeps from my breasts and covers my belly. The water is bracing, and I cannot tolerate it for long.

Devoid of the armor, Calden wades into the river beside me, only far deeper until he can submerge himself, washing off the sweat, grime, and blood. His eyes are upon me as I make for the shore.

Where once they held warmth, now he has become a stranger to me, and I, a stranger to him.

I don't make it to the bank before he scoops me up and hoists me out of the water.

"Please!" I protest. "You will hurt yourself!"

"I think the damage is already done, woman," he says, a coolness in his tone that I have not heard before, and that makes me think he's talking about far more than just the wounds that litter his body. He swings me around, placing me upon his back. I do not hesitate to put my arms around him and press closely, my nipples unbearably sensitive as they brush against his muscular back. My thighs are spread wide around his beastly body, and to my shame, not only does water dampen his coat, but my pussy is assuredly hot for other reasons.

"Hold on tightly," he says. "We have much ground to cover."

I do, pressing my cheek to his warm back, drawing his beautiful scent into my lungs, and surreptitiously petting his firm waist under the pretext of getting settled. Our bodies are damp from the river and a little slick where we press together.

Why did I ever run? That's right—because the pain of him not loving me back is worse than any other.

With his armor distributed among the other centaurs, we set off into the forest again at a fast pace. I have lost all bearings with all the many journeys I have made. I wonder if we are heading back to his village on the shores of the lake, whether Lila and Chastity will be waiting, worried for their mates and me.

Or perhaps he is bringing me somewhere else, wanting to be rid of me and taking me to my former home and Karl.

"You took what was mine," he said. No, I cannot believe he would send me away. He is the noblest, most wondrous creature in all the world and only seeks to protect me, despite how much of a nuisance I am.

To my surprise, we stop in a human village, one I do not know. Axton speaks with the local lord while we wait on the outskirts to the villagers' interest. We are given lodgings over a hay barn, mostly empty at this time of year, where we are to bed down for the night. The villagers are kindly and curious as they bring food and ale. There is even a soft homespun woolen blanket for me. Calden takes the blanket on my behalf from the woman who offers it up. He does not, however, give it to me.

I look longingly at the blanket in his hands and then shyly up at his face.

"You may have it for sleeping," he says. "But it is not cold and you will not have it yet."

As his hooded gaze lowers to my weeping breasts, I nibble on my lower lip. "If I might have leave to clean myself in the nearby stream, milord."

His lips twitch the tiniest amount at my use of a title, and my fool heart flutters with the hope that things are not entirely broken and he might be softening toward me. Then he shakes his head, and his nostrils flare. His beautiful white hair makes a halo around his face. "You'll have some food, woman." He points to the bowl of stew set aside on the nearby haybale before turning and trotting over to talk to Axton.

Only I don't want food, and my tummy recoils at the mere thought. I pick up the bowl and sit, finding a corner a little away from the others, partially hidden from view by a few old bales of hay. I stare at the food, which is considerably better than the slop I was given in the stables of Dires End, although I still don't want it.

When Calden returns, I have still eaten none and merely moved it around with my spoon. He looks from me to the food, lips tightening before he clicks his tongue in disapproval. He turns about, spreading the small amount of hay to make a bed of sorts, then settles down and crooks his finger toward me. "Come here, woman."

I shake my head.

"Do not make me come and fetch you, lest you find yourself in greater trouble than you already are."

I rise sullenly, feeling much like a scolded child, aware of my foolishness and not knowing where this sudden willfulness arises from. After all he has just done for me, I should be good and obedient. I should beg him for forgiveness, yet I don't know where to begin.

The bowl is put down in an act of rebellion, then I move and attempt to settle without touching him.

He snorts out a whinny and snags me around the waist to my squeal of protest.

No words are spoken, but I feel every inch of his glorious body where it presses to mine. The sun is sinking, casting the barn into shadows. Beyond the small wall of bales, the other centaurs talk quietly.

My first sob comes out of nowhere, and I gulp his scent down and bury my nose against his warm chest.

"Steady, Hope, I have got you," he says. "What nonsense was this about? You agreed to be mine for a moon month. Have I not treated you well? Have I not cared for you and ensured you were safe?"

"Yes!" I say, hearing the deep hurt in his words.

"Then what madness would cause you to run like this?"

Only I can't tell him how terrified I am by my feelings for him. How could I? "Take me back to Melwood."

The moment the words leave my mouth, I know I have gone too far, but the longer I am with Calden, the more I fall for him. When the moon month is up, he will put me aside.

"I will do no such thing. When was the last time you ate?" he demands.

"I don't remember. I-I don't have any appetite."

"You are suffering unnecessarily, foolish woman. Your moon month is assuredly not up, and until then, I shall take full responsibility for you."

I nod, knowing I have no choice. His gentle care for me, nothing but an indebted lass, is a thousand times more than my husband ever did. My eyes shift unerringly toward his cock, and my tummy rumbles, seeing it has thrust fully from the sheath. I swallow against my dust dry throat. All I can think about is how I tended to him before all this began. How it tasted...and what came after. "May I..." I can't believe I am asking for this. My face flushes. "Please, may I tend to you?"

"No." His tone is harsh. "You have been very naughty and are not worthy."

I sob, his words cutting me deeply.

"You will eat the food provided like a good girl. When I am satisfied you are behaving, I will consider your request. Your mischief might require a second moon month of service."

"Oh, it does," I say, and my tears dry up in a flash, despite knowing my heart will break twice as hard. I want him. I want to be good for him, and then perhaps he will allow me to stay...but if I misbehave, will that force him to keep me longer?

His eyes narrow. "What are you plotting, Hope?"

I swallow. "Nothing!"

"Hmmm. If you promise to be good, mayhap you may tend me now. I don't like that you are not eating properly, although I'm loath to reward your mischief."

"I am going to be so good!" I say while intending to do the opposite. A plan lays out before me—I will be good until it nears the end of my debt, when I shall be bad. Not a running away sort of bad, but something else sufficient to see him extend my debt. Mayhap if I do this long enough, he will forget all about sending me away altogether. I all but fall over his forelegs and close my hands around his cock with a sob of joy. He is leaking copiously, and I lap enthusiastically at the weeping tip.

"Steady, sweet Hope," he says, gathering my hair so he can watch what I do. "You will make yourself ill by gorging like this."

I slow, tempering my enthusiasm only as much as I think I must to satisfy him, cupping his heavy balls and moaning as I note how full they are. Already, my pussy is weeping as the taste hits my belly…and thinking about the rapture after as it works upon my body. I am nearly climaxing from the thought alone.

"Good girl," he encourages, parting his stifle so I can fully get to him. "That's better, isn't it? Use your tongue." He groans softly. "There, I can see a little color in your cheeks. Is that what you needed, my love?"

My heart swells when he uses that endearment. I squeeze the fat head of his cock into my mouth and suckle as best as I can while running my hands over the hot, silken length.

"I'm going to come for you, love. I can sense your need is great and there is sure to be a lot."

I suck harder and brace myself, humming in anticipation.

He groans, and a great rush of hot, spicy seed floods my mouth. I gulp, choke a little, and gulp some more, running my hands the length, ensuring I get every drop before cupping his balls and fondling them until he rewards me with the final, sweetest gush. My tummy instantly feels better, full, and content.

I sigh as he draws me back into his arms, only my contentment does not last more than a moment. A strange urgency rises within me, and I grow restless, kicking out my legs until he clamps an arm around my waist and pins me to him, keeping me still.

"Hush," he murmurs, his lips against my hair.

Only I don't hush, and a kind of madness grips me as I feel the flush of heat. I sink my teeth into the strong column of his throat and bite hard.

He grunts and reaches to cup the back of my head, holding me tighter, just in time, as a storm gathers me up. I moan into his flesh, biting, tasting blood, and not even caring that I am little more than an animal as I hump my pussy against his firm tummy and rub my sensitive breasts against his chest. The climax rips through me, stronger and more powerful than I have experienced before, setting my body spasming in erotic waves and my mind spinning into heaven.

"I have got you, love," he says. "My naughty charge, before the Goddess you are assuredly mine."

Pleasure courses through me, making me twitch and groan, making my pussy and breasts weep.

There is an intense clenching in my pussy as I squeeze over nothing. My lips pop off as a terrible openness assaults me. "Oh!" I think my pussy is broken. Maybe I shouldn't do this again?

"Are you well?" he asks.

"Yes," I say softly, but I remember how he is injured and how I just bit him like a savage. "Are you? Did… I-I'm sorry I bit you. I don't know what came over me."

"Don't mind it," he says. "A natural reaction to the stress. Can you sleep now? Can you be good for me tonight, or must I bind you, lest you run off again?"

My stomach performs a slow dip at the mention of him binding me. I think he notices because his nostrils flare. "I think some reins might be in order when we arrive home tomorrow. It will go some way to settling you into your moon debt."

"Reins," I whisper, thinking about how the lass on the saddle had a collar with thin straps leading from it to her nipples, forming reins the centaur mounting her held in his hand.

He brushes the hair back from my hot cheek, running his fingers down over my throat, all the way to my breast, where he cups the weight before squeezing my nipple. I suck a sharp breath in, trying

143

to be still, lest he stop. "I think these pretty plump tits would look beautiful in reins. It would please me greatly to do so. Are they sensitive?" He pinches and rolls the tip, bringing a whimper to my lips, and I nod helplessly, wishing desperately for him to tend them. "We shall also cap them to stop them weeping all the time. I dare say they will grow quite sore, swelling with your sweet milk, but I shall tend them when I have time and that will provide you with some relief."

Goddess! They are sore enough now when they can weep. I cannot imagine how they might feel if he caps them. How would he even do that? Yet even as I fear this, my pussy clenches sharply and the terrible openness blooms anew.

His face grows stern in the fading light as he toys with my nipple, making me hot and urgent all over again. "*If* you are good. However, if there is any mischief, rest assured, I shall not tend to them at all. Especially if I find you removing the cap. I will take the strap to your naughty bottom and keep you bound until you learn to better behave."

"I'll be good," I promise, pushing my breast into his hand wantonly, hoping he might suckle them right now.

"Okay then." He releases my nipple, leaving it throbbing with need. "Settle down and rest like a good girl, and we shall see what comes to be. You have already earned yourself another moon month of debt. Don't make it any worse, or you may never leave."

"I'll be good, milord," I squeak out, even as I decide I shall do the exact opposite.

Despite the aches in my body and the terrible events that have passed, I am the happiest I have ever been. Plotting what I must do to ensure he never lets me go, I drift into sleep.

CHAPTER NINETEEN

Calden

My woman is plotting, I have no doubt about it, as we journey back to our home. What, is yet to be revealed.

"I do not want you," she said back in Dires End. What had I been expecting? She ran from me, took a horse, and rode away. Then last night, she fed from me so sweetly. I am torn between hope and fear that I am a fool. My heart is sore that she ran away at all, and I cannot readily reconcile the nightmares of the past few days. Grimm and his fallen centaur fortress are no place for a sweet woman. Their life is one of constant conflict, living as they do besides the broken portal through which all manner of horrors emerge. It makes for hard centaurs and a harsh environment all around. They use their human charges frequently and lustily, by all accounts, and would surely break one so gentle as Hope.

Still, she ran from me, and although I want to believe she might come to care for me, I cannot say how her feelings are now. Perhaps I am merely the lesser of two evils?

I tell myself I should let her go, but how can I when her body responds to mine? Her lush tits and weeping pussy, which I have yet to taste directly, leave me in a state of heightened arousal and near maddening need. Little wonder my brain is fogged and I cannot think straight. I am confident the lass craves my cock, but I also need her love.

As we test our fit, I will tolerate many things, but I will not tolerate her running and putting herself in danger. I am not one for drawing out stress by warning her of her upcoming punishment, but one is assuredly due—the kind that will ensure she never runs again.

As the shores of the lake come into view, I feel her small hands tighten on my waist.

"We're home," she says, her voice sleepy, for night is falling and it has been a long day.

Her words find a chink in the sorrowful place inside. "Aye, Hope, we are."

"Hail, Axton!" the two centaurs on sentry call, thumping their spear butts against the ground. The young centaur lad, Peter, darts off into the village, calling out. Soon, the village is roused from early evening activity to greet us. Lila and Chastity come running until Gael and Axton both holler for them to walk. It stirs a chuckle from my lips and instills a lightness in my heart. I know well the feeling of protectiveness toward a charge, especially Axton, for his mate is plump with child. The two women are gathered up into arms, where they receive their due kisses and cuddles, assuring themselves, as do the other villagers, that mates and loved ones are returned whole.

Lila's head pops up and turns toward Hope…soon followed by Chastity's wriggling and demands to get down and check upon her friend.

Axton keeps his mate in hand and shares a look with me. "Not now, love," he says. "Hope and Calden have much to work through. Rest assured the lass is safe."

I incline my head in gratitude. There is indeed much I will need to be working through. It might be some time before Hope will be drinking tea with her friends. Leaving the relieved swell of villagers, I trot on past them for home. Here, I set Hope on the high table before putting on a lamp. "Are you hungry? Thirsty?" I ask.

She blushes a pretty shade of pink and looks everywhere but me. I step over to her and use my fingers to tip her chin, letting my face show how serious this moment is. "There will be none of that. You'll be getting the broth, and assuredly, I shall suffer as much as you. You shall not be taking tea with Chastity and Lila, either, not until I am satisfied. You are in my moon debt until I decide otherwise, given you have run."

"I'm sorry," she says. "I wish I hadn't. I don't know why I did."

Except I don't believe her. Not the sorrow part, which is plain and true, but the part about not knowing why she fled. I wonder if perhaps I need to go even slower with her, despite the opposite feeling most right. Tears spill down her cheeks, and I brush them away with my thumbs. "There, it is not my desire to upset you, but there is much we must discuss, as Axton said."

She nods, swiftly dashing the tears from her cheeks. "Will we still sleep together upon your bed?" she asks solemnly.

"Yes, we will."

"Then I shall suffer everything else willingly." She lowers her voice to a scandalized whisper. "Even the broth."

I snort out a laugh despite my determination to remain firm, and picking her up, take her to my bed. I cuddle her, for I cannot help myself, although I do not let my hands stray to her pretty tits, nor her pussy, which is slick where she presses up against the beastly part of my body. Still, she is here now, in my arms, where she is right and perfect.

Tomorrow, I predict a bumpy ride.

I leave home early, but I don't lock the door. Although I have a strong urge to do as much, I'm not that cruel. Instead, I instruct Peter to watch the house. She may go to the river to clean and go about her business, but she will assuredly not be wandering off. Satisfied that no mischief will occur in my absence, I go to meet our resident carpenter, Dorn.

Dorn is an older centaur with graying whiskers and a wild head of hair. He is busy at work already, although the sun has barely risen. "Hail, Calden," he calls, grinning broadly. "I thought I would hear from you today."

My smile is rueful. The whole damn herd will be up in our business now. Not that I can blame them. "Are they ready?"

He nods and motions me over to the far corner of his workshop, where he pulls a cloth aside to reveal a beautiful mounting bench.

"Aye, that is a stunning piece of craftsmanship." I rest my hand against the saddle, noting the smooth wood and how soft the leather is. I have never been with a human in this way, and the sudden heightened awareness is hard to ignore. I have yet to touch Hope intimately, but that is about to change.

"Go ahead," he says. "Try out the settings."

I pull the lever on the side, tilting the saddle for ease of access.

"Bob brought these over for you." Dorn unwraps a cloth bundle upon the bench, revealing a set of butter-soft leather cuffs for wrists and ankles, a collar, and reins. There is also a smaller package in a suede pouch. I resist opening it, certain my body will go into riot the moment I see what lies within, and decide I shall open it when I am with Hope.

"My deepest gratitude to you both," I say. "These are fine indeed."

"Happy to," he replies. "Just glad to have the lass back safe. It's not always an easy road when a centaur takes a human mate. Rene and I went through some back and forth afore we settled. It's a lot for a human lass to accept. It's not just about the physical differences, although to be sure that is much of it and daunting on both sides, for no centaur wants to harm a woman in coupling and no woman thinks her body can accept such a beastly male. My Rene was worried I didn't love her, of all things." He chuckles softly. "As if I weren't smitten with her from the moment our eyes met. She got some fool notion about me casting her aside at the end of the month. She laughs about it now, and it seems foolish upon reflection." He steps to his right and pulls another cloth aside to reveal a tall chair.

I step forward to admire it, even as my mind whirls with all he just said. Is it possible Hope thinks I would cast her aside? Is that what this nonsense is about? It seems too simple a solution to what feels like a complex situation.

Do I move too fast or too slow? If I announce my feelings for her, would it settle us or drive her to run again?

"When can you bring them around?" I ask.

"I can have the lads drop them around tomorrow, if that works for you? Just need to fit the braces at the bottom, and I'll need a couple of lads to help me bring it around and to securely bolt it into place. The stool you asked for is ready now." He gestures to the open doors at the back that lead down to a cobbled outbuilding. "I'll get it brought over directly."

I nod. "My thanks, that would be perfect."

When Hope first mentioned a stool, I thought it an insult to a woman I wanted as my mate. Now, it will have another purpose as I settle her into her new life. As I leave the carpenter's workshop, my thoughts center on the cuffs, collar, and reins in my hands, and the smaller item held within the soft suede pouch.

CHAPTER TWENTY

Hope

I wake alone and confused by the softness underneath me. Then everything comes rushing back, and I sit up with a start.

I'm here, back with Calden, in his bed. Relief and overwhelming gratitude assault me as I suck in deep breaths. The nightmare is over for me, but I cannot help but reflect upon the poor women who must endure within Dires End. Perhaps endure is not the right word, for Summer was very much reconciled to her place and position. It is not my place to judge, but I understand that to be touched thusly by anyone but Calden would break my heart.

There is no hope for me. I am besotted with the male. He was all I could think about after the first time he saved me, and now, he is the center of my world.

Pushing the soft covers back, I rise from the bed. A hide dress is waiting for me on the little hook beside the door. It makes me a little teary that he kept it. With trembling fingers, I collect the dress and slip it on. Calden remains absent, so I decide I shall go down to the river to wash and complete my business. He said I couldn't visit Chastity or Lila, but the memory of their worried faces when we arrived last eve compounds my sense of guilt.

Outside, I find the young centaur lad, Peter, standing beside the stone wall that lines the vegetable plot.

"Oh!" I say unnecessarily.

"I'm to watch you," he says, grinning. "But not too closely. Calden threatened to box my ears if I watched you bathing."

I blush, which is ridiculous, given that he is only a lad, and hasten to my business.

I give myself a talking to as I wash in the river, determined to make good on my promise to Calden. Distracted by my musings, I turn back from the river, naked and dripping...and scream.

Calden chuckles.

Goddess, he is a resplendent male and simply stunning when his face shines with laughter. His beautiful white hair falls in waves around his handsome face, while his folded arms draw my focus to the bulging muscles in his arms and lower, to the beastly part of him. A centaur is hard to reconcile as a being, for they are strange and compelling...and huge. He is unquestionably huge and powerful beyond human measure.

My eyes flash to meet his, realizing I have been perusing him in a most unseemly way, probably with my mouth open and all but drooling with my lust, yet he only appears amused. A heavy throb kicks off low in my womb, and my breasts ache, desperate for his tending. It has been so long since I felt his hands and mouth upon me there, I might go a little crazy from my needs.

Only he is too much male, and I am nothing but a plump lass whose husband wanted her only for her money.

"What was that about?" he asks, eyes narrowing upon me.

"I... Nothing," I say inadequately. How do I put to words these feelings that assault my mind? Worries about my attractiveness to him seem paltry in light of all that has come to pass, yet they are no less important or valid. I want to blurt the words out, to ask outright if he finds me comely, but I fear him either laughing at my nonsense or the awkwardness when he searches for a polite way to avoid answering. He is a noble centaur, and I can well imagine him trying to shield my feelings, now that I think about it.

"You are too much in your head, woman," he finally says. He trots over to the nearby tree, snagging my dress from where it lies over a branch. I swallow, instinctively knowing he is not about to offer it to me. "Come," he says, crooking his finger to me. "Time for your punishment."

My stomach performs a low dip, and I hasten to his side, lest I incur further wrath. I squeak as he scoops me up, naked and damp, into his arm. "I want my dress!"

"You shall not be wearing your dress again for a long time," he all but growls at me, trotting through the village back to his home, while I wriggle and blush a deep shade of red.

He proceeds straight into the home and kicks the door shut with a thud before dropping me to my feet. He spins me around and lands a sound spank on my ass.

"Goddess, your ass is a test of a male's lust. Get into position over the table, woman."

My ass stings, and I rub the smarting flesh as I glance back, seeking to check I heard him right.

His grin is all teeth and confirms his words. "I shall enjoy this, but after your mischief, I shall not suffer a lick of guilt."

My feet make a patter as I hurry over to the table, clamber up on the thick beam, and lay my torso over the sturdy wooden surface, not even shamed by my eagerness to have his big hands upon me any way I can. I press my cheek to the top and slip my fingers into the grooves. My heart races wildly, and already, my pussy feels slick.

His hooves thud against the compacted earth floor as he moves off and returns.

I start as he trails a strip of leather down my back until it settles against my ass. "Plump and pretty," he mutters. "A vision of femininity, all laid out for me... Now, open your pretty thighs, love."

Heat blooms in my cheeks at being so exposed. The unmistakable splat makes my pussy clench. Goodness, I know his cock is leaking again. Even after all I have done, he still desires me, and my giddy heart sings.

I hear a soft clatter, and my eyes spring open to find the strap placed beside my face. His hands go to my hips, big broad hands skimming possessively over flesh, thumbs pressing deep near to my pussy, pulling me gently open and relaxing, only to pull again.

Oh, what is he doing to me? It makes me feel so shockingly open. His thumbs are so close to my pussy. The feeling of being drawn apart and exposed before him makes my pussy weep, wanting his touch closer to my throbbing core.

"Good girl," he croons softly. "The strap will sting a great deal, but it will help you better submit to our ways."

I know not what he is talking about, but my breathing turns a little choppy. All I can think about is how close he is to my core and how good it would feel if he finally touched me there. Suddenly, I am convinced I am ready for his thick cock, as monstrous as it is, for it would fill this terrible, empty ache.

"Brace yourself, Hope. This will be a stern punishment. Afterward, your pretty nipples will be capped while you go about your chores." ·

I whimper and swear my breasts swell at his declaration that he shall cap them.

The strap is gathered up, and the first crack as it meets my ass stirs a gasp from me. It sounds worse than it feels, although it leaves a residual sting. The next is a little firmer, lifting me from the table. I close my eyes and bite my lower lip, determined not to make a fuss.

Crack.

"You will not put yourself in danger like that again."

Crack.

"You will be good and obedient for me."

Crack.

"You have already earned yourself a second moon month of debt."

He pauses to pet the stinging flesh, and it is all I can do to be still.

Crack!

"I searched for you the moment I found you were missing. Every able member of the herd did until we found where you had gone. What if I had failed? What if I had lost the challenge? What if Grimm had refused me the right to challenge, and we had been forced to war with them?"

Crack. Crack. Crack!

The tears fall as the sting rises to a burn, and I accept all my due. I ran away, putting not only myself in danger, but all the herd. I cannot believe that he was looking for me all this time, not only Calden but also the other warriors. Worse, while they were looking for me, they were not protecting mates and loved ones. How the guilt assaults me, thinking about Lila and Chastity worrying for their mates, and both of them with child. My foolishness could have cost them and the villagers dearly. It is easy to see how the situation might have gone so much worse with hindsight.

"I am sorry," I sob out. "I won't run again. I promise." The strap is dropped, and I am turned over and gathered against his warm chest, where I cry all over him. "I won't do anything like that again. I swear."

His big hands now soothe me. My bottom throbs like a thousand bee stings, but I don't even care.

"There, the matter is over now. You took your punishment like a good girl for me. Still, there will be no more feeding, save for broth, nor shall you be visiting your friends until I am fully satisfied of your penance. There will be light chores for you to do around the home. Likewise, clothing is a privilege you will need to earn."

I nod eagerly, ready to pay my dues so that we might move on. I cannot bear the thought of disappointing Calden again.

"Now," he says ominously, settling me back upon the table. "It is time for you to be prepared in a way that pleases me."

"Okay," I say, scrubbing the dampness from my cheeks and watching as he gathers a cloth wrapped bundle and opens it beside me on the table.

I suck in a sharp breath as I see the beautiful collar and cuffs. They are made of tan leather and appear fine and delicate against his big, rough hands. There are also two long reins, which he pushes aside, instead selecting the collar.

"It will please me for you to wear these, and only these," he says. "A centaur is a possessive male. You are mine until the debt is paid. Given you ran and called into question my mastery over you, I need this, need to mark you as mine."

I dare to glance up, noticing how dark his eyes are, hearing a couple of telltale splats and squirming where my hot bottom touches the table. "Please," I say, lifting my hair, shameless and eager for him to put them upon me.

My breasts quiver as he settles the collar into place, taking his time to test the fit and ensure it is not too tight. When he moves his hands away, it feels like he is holding me there, and I like it very much. Next comes the cuffs upon my wrists. Again, he takes his time, ensuring they are snug but still comfortable. Then comes my ankles, and I must bite my lip to stifle my groan when his eyes stray to the juncture of my thighs, where my pussy is exposed to his lusty gaze as he lifts me to fit each cuff.

By the time he is done with his erotic claiming, I am a mess of need and my breasts weep copiously.

155

"There," he says, stroking a single finger under the swell of my breast and scooping up the clear stickiness before taking it to his mouth and sucking with a groan. "You look beautiful, Hope. I should have claimed you thusly at the start, and this foolishness might not have happened, hmmm?"

He doesn't wait for my answer. Instead, he tips out the contents of a smaller suede pouch.

"Goddess!" I mutter when I see the strange metal disks that are ornate like a brooch might be. Instantly, I know what they are, but it is not them that I linger on, but the bulbous-shaped metal plug with a long, soft gray tail attached. Everything inside clenches as I realize what it is, even as I question how or why.

I glance up, finding him watching not the things revealed…but my reaction.

When my breasts first started to weep, I was worried I was broken. Like many changes I have experienced within myself, I realize it is simply the potency of a centaur acting upon my human body. I have long believed and trusted in the Goddess. Of late, my trust has waned, and I plant my troubles firmly at this door. Now, I shall follow her ways in acceptance and submit fully to my centaur's needs.

I have no choice anyway, and I find I like that. There is freedom in my new mindset. The stinging of my bottom reminds me that I am here and alive, that time is short and precious, and that to waste any is the highest form of sin. I have earned myself another moon month. I shall not squander this time, for even if his feelings for me never grow and this one-sided love is all I have, I must cherish it and store it up to last the rest of my earthly life.

His big hands settle upon my waist and slowly skim up toward my quivering breasts. I moan a little as he cups them, rough thumbs brushing over the engorged nipples and lighting a fire that passes all the way to my clit.

"Are they sensitive, love?"

I nod, nibbling upon my lower lip.

He tests the weight, groaning as he sees how heavy they are.

"If I am good, can I tend to you afterward?" I blurt out.

"No," he says, eyes turning hooded as he pinches my nipples roughly. "I have already said as much. You will accept this as part of your penance, and to help you to better learn your place within my care and debt. As will the plug and tail, which will please me to place in your bottom."

I swallow nervously, torn between sharp arousal as he twists and pets my nipples and shock at the depravity of the male.

"I have it on good authority," he continues, driving my body to a frenzy and drugging my mind with his deep voice and bold words, "that querulous women soon learn their place with the aid of a tail."

Goddess help me. Calden is scandalous. I cannot begin to understand why my breath turns choppy, and I become convinced that I shall climax from his petting of my nipples alone.

His nostrils flare, and his hands suddenly still. "Do not come, woman. You are assuredly not getting any reward this day."

I tremble violently, while he holds his big capable hands against my breasts, cupping them, fingers pinching lightly over my stiff nipples and making me half crazy with the need for more.

"Why did you leave?"

"I... What?" I try to scramble for an answer to his sudden question, blinking as I try and fail to find ground.

"It is a simple question, Hope. Do you doubt my commitment to keeping you safe?"

I flounder for an answer as he applies the first cap to my breast. I splutter a few curses and nonsense words as he tightens it over my nipple. He must anticipate I will struggle, for he plants an arm around my waist and pins my arms to my side.

"Goddess! What?! Oh, it is too tight!"

I get a spank to my thigh for my mischief, and he clips something I can't quite see, doubling the sensation of tightness.

"Ummm!!! Oh!"

"You are making a lot of fuss about this." He tugs upon the ornate contraption that torments me to a maddening level. "Breathe," he continues, pulling and twisting it and making all the sensations spiral until I cannot decide whether I will lose my mind or climax.

I do neither, and with his jaw locked and eyes dark, he moves to the other side to perform the same torture.

"Beautiful," he murmurs, while I gasp and wriggle and convince myself I will expire if he leaves these on me all day. "Now, I will apply the plug to your naughty bottom, which will help to keep you focused while you work."

"I don't need further foc—Ouch!" I am picked up and placed face down, and a sharp spank is applied to my upturned bottom.

"Quiet down, Hope. It pleases me to do this. It hasn't escaped my notice that you did not answer my question. Mayhap you will feel more like talking once you are wearing a pretty tail. Reach your hands back and pull your ass cheeks open for me, so I can better see where this needs to go."

I throw a wild look over my shoulder, but another sharp spank is all the motivation I need. This is not open to discussion. With a huff of frustration, I reach my hands back and, to my utmost humiliation, pull my ass cheeks open. I thought my sense of shame was utterly broken, but the wicked centaur finds new heights, and all the while, the sensation builds in my nipples like his fingers are still petting me. He moves off, hooves thudding, and returns with an earthen jar, which he places upon the table beside me. He pops off the cork lid and dips his fingers in.

"Good girl, has anyone touched you here before?"

"No!"

"Hmm," he says, and the unmistakable splats of his lust are like rain upon the floor. A slick finger slowly presses into my puckered back entrance, setting me squirming and wriggling anew as all the sensitive nerves flare to life. "Many centaurs do not enjoy such pleasure, but I have often thought about it. It is your own fault for having such a beautifully plump ass." He pumps slowly, with a single finger. "How does that feel?"

"I don't like it," I wail.

"I don't believe you, Hope. The scent of your lust near saturates the air. You are taking to this beautifully, my filthy, lusty woman. With some training, you might even accept the tip of my cock in here." My protest turns to a moan as he forces a second finger inside, creating a deep burn as he scissors his fingers before pumping slowly again. "Does that feel good, love?"

"It feels depraved!"

His chuckle is low and dark. Oh, he is very much enjoying what he does. Only I cannot lie to myself. I am panting with arousal as the dark stretching sets my body aflame. My eyes roll back in my head, and my breath hitches. No, I cannot come like this?

"I think that is enough," he says, stopping. "I don't want you to come yet. Better you spend the day thinking about the answer to the question you are reluctant to give."

Question? What question?

I cannot gather wits to recall where I am, never mind questions, and even that much flies out of my head as Calden presses the cool metal plug against my back entrance. "Good girl, just relax for me and let me do this." The stretch is alarming, burning, and frightening, but then it pops in, making me feel full and aroused all at once. "Beautiful. I'm just going to work it in and out to ensure it is fitted comfortably."

My fingers tremble where I hold my ass cheeks parted. Making me hold myself open thusly, while he works the thick plug in and out of me, is surely the darkest, most twisted pleasure. Where did my noble centaur go?

But oh, how I love this dark version of Calden and all the terrible torment he lays upon my body. My pussy weeps, slick trickling down the tops of my thighs as he plays with the plug. Soon, it doesn't burn, just a twisty kind of pleasure that makes my ass tingle. I wonder what it might be like, if, as he said, he were to work the flared tip of his monstrous cock into me there.

"You can let go now, love. Put your hands beside your face and keep them still."

The relief in moving my hands away is short-lived. The plug pops in fully, and Calden grasps the tail, pulling it and then releasing it, making the plug work against the entrance of my ass over and over again. My throbbing nipples work in tandem with the dark pleasure building in my ass.

"Goddess, your lush, ripe body is a test of the highest order," he says roughly. "I think it might better help you to settle if I could work some of my seed into your most intimate place. Would you like that? Can you be good and still for me while I do this?"

I am quivering with excitement. My whole body is lost under a sensual storm.

"Please," I say, not fully understanding what I want, only knowing I need something to relieve this abominable pressure. "I want you to."

The sudden clatter as his front hooves hit the table is shocking. They skitter a little over the surface before slamming into the grooves beside my head. The feel of his beastly body towering over me sends a sharp shot of fear and excitement racing through me. The soft fur of his belly brushes against my ass, catching the tail, making me tremble. Goodness, is this why there are slots upon the table?

"Tell me you want this," he demands. "Tell me you want my seed."

"Oh, I do," I whisper helplessly. He barely touches me, but the sensation of being surrounded by his power, along with the plug in my ass and my capped nipples, have me teetering on the brink. Then I feel his fat, flared cock head sliding over my swollen folds, brushing back and forth, catching my clit with every gentle rock. The flared tip is slick and mobile and slides against me in such a way that my entire pussy thrums. It almost feels like it *moves* against me, seeking and sucking over my flesh.

"Tell me to come inside you, Hope."

"Please, come, I want you to come. I want you inside me."

His flared cock catches the entrance to my pussy on the next pass.

I wriggle, alarmed by the monstrous stretch, sweat popping out across the surface of my skin. He lowers a little weight, pinning me against the table, stilling me, his cock throbbing against my pussy.

He groans, and a hot flood fills me, pulsing, hot, dripping down my thighs and all the way to the floor.

Goddess, he has come inside me. I have taken him a little way. I am full and dripping with centaur seed.

"I want to come!" I announce, not even caring if this is forward of me. If only he would move a little, it would assuredly happen.

He chuckles, a deep raspy sound that warms my heart, even as it ticks me off.

"Oh! This is no laughing matter. Do not dare to leave me like this all day."

He slips out, hooves clattering as he dismounts. A great flood of cum splats against the floor, and I wail my displeasure, throwing a hand back like I might have a hope of stemming the deluge.

The spank to my bottom is unwelcome, and I hiss at the male who has left me hanging in the worst of ways. All sense of humility

161

flees me in the wake of my needs.

He turns me over, planting my ass against the edge of the table with the tail hanging down. "You are losing a lot, naughty human," he murmurs, hooded eyes locked upon my drenched pussy, then his big hand is there, cupping me intimately. "Let me help you with that."

Thick fingers scoop up the leaking seed and thrust it back in. I have no shame, letting my legs fall open, panting as I stare down at what Calden does, feeling him press inside me, watching the intense expression on his face.

"Oh!" I gasp as his rough fingertips scrape over something sensitive inside. "What?"

"A slick gland... You are indeed changing." His eyes narrow, seeming to take on a savage edge as he pins me firmly against the table and proceeds to explore the sensitive spot. "You are tight," he says. "And will need considerable training before you will take me fully here." My jaw turns slack as I twitch and gasp and try to decide if his rough petting is too much or not enough. My nipples throb, as does my plugged ass and pussy. Everything gathers together into a glorious bundle of bliss. "Come if you need to, my filthy, needy love."

His thumb presses against my clit as his fingers circle the sensitive bundle deep inside.

I come, gasping, spasming, riding his hand, heat flushing over my body as I tumble into rapture.

"Good girl," he rumbles. "How beautiful you look coming just for me."

As the last throes of the climax leave me, I fall utterly limp.

His soft tutting rouses me, and I blink up at him. "Looks like your ass isn't the only place that needs to be plugged."

CHAPTER TWENTY ONE

Calden

That did not go quite to plan, I reflect as I help her clean up, check her capped nipples, which she complains vigorously about, and then set her to preparing our broth...so she has something to occupy herself. I find it hard to tear myself away, seeing her thoroughly marked as mine with a collar, cuffs, and cute fluffy tail, but I left a small stool outside earlier and now fetch it in so she might have access to the table.

"Oh!" she says on seeing the stool in my hand. "You got me a stool!"

She promptly bursts into tears, which worries me that I might have either broken the lass with my near rutting or insulted her with this lowly offering.

"I'm so happy," she wails, holding the stool like a cherished gift rather than a small wooden block not even made with any particular finesse.

It takes a while to calm her down. By this point, I am near

insensible with my need to rut her, distracted by her plump, capped tits and the tail that wiggles enticingly as she puts the stool before the table, where she begins preparations of the broth.

I leave, charging straight for the lake, and douse myself in the frigid water for several long minutes until I can cool my ardor enough to go about my business without my cock out. I leave the water intending to inform Dorn to deliver the saddling station with all haste. The table is no place to take a lass for the first time. Given her tightness, she will need to be securely strapped down so I might safely rut her.

No, I cannot think about that, or I will need to go to the fucking lake again!

I am interrupted from my musing by the centaur lad, Peter.

"Gael is looking for you, Calden!" he calls. "Said it was urgent."

Frowning, for I cannot imagine what is urgent, I change direction and head for his home.

Here I find both Chastity and Lila, along with their mates, standing before Gael's home, wringing their hands, pink-cheeked, and neither of them meeting my eyes. Lila's pale face is blotchy, and her eyes are red-rimmed from tears.

"What is this about?" I ask.

"Go on, Lila," Gael says. "Tell Calden what transpired."

"The day before Hope ran, she saw the saddle," Lila says. "She was curious about it. I…"

"Keep going," Gael says sternly.

"I was worried I would get into trouble." Lila sends a furtive glance toward Chastity, who squeezes her hand as if in support. "She said you didn't have one, and I said you had no need for one on account of your never sharing intimacy with any human lass." Her face turns bright red. "I was too busy worrying about the trouble I would be in if she told. I wasn't thinking straight. I thought at first that she was only shocked. Well, she was shocked for sure, but after, it wasn't shock, more a distant kind of sadness." My nostrils flare, for I can sense where this is going. "Afterward, she asked about…about how it might be between a lass and a centaur." Her face now blazes as she shrugs helplessly. "I said it was a great pleasure…and then I got scared in case I was terrifying the lass, for she is sweet and I already love her so, and I said something about how you would never do that to her…and that was when she said she needed to be getting back to duties at home."

My chest heaves, and a heaviness settles behind my eyes.

"I don't think she was scared at all, not at first, only curious, but after all my babbling, she looked so sad and everything I said only made it worse, and then she ran. Oh! I think I made her think you didn't care for her, that you didn't like a human lass in that way!" She bursts out crying.

Chastity rubs her shoulder, both women sending nervous looks my way, as well they should.

Only it is not all upon their shoulders. I recall how excited Hope was about the stool. Yesterday, when I mentioned her earning herself an additional moon debt because she fled, her eyes had lit up.

The only conclusion I can draw is that she genuinely wants to be with me, and that she is indeed ready for all I want and need.

"Do not burden yourselves with this, Lila," I say. "I am not angry with you, only angry at myself. I was trying to go slow with Hope, not to rush her. I had the saddle ready a week ago, but it is a lot for a woman new to centaurs to take. Only Hope did not come and talk to me. Instead, she ran and put herself in danger."

"I let her in the home!" Lila wails.

"Aye," Gael agrees.

"You both did," Axton adds ominously. "When you were expressly told not to, for reasons such as this. There will be punishment for that."

I snort out a laugh when they both send worried looks and

whisper, "broth," in scandalized unison.

"I need to go," I say, my mind five steps ahead of my body and scrambling to work out what needs to happen in between.

"About time," Axton says, and I hear the smile in his voice. Only I am already turning on the spot and trotting back toward Dorn. I need the saddle…and I need Hope in it.

Hope

Today is both the best and worst of days, as I gather the ingredients for the broth. Not only do I have to suffer broth, but I must prepare it as well, yet I do so joyfully, given Calden bought me a stool.

I weep every time I think about it, which is ridiculous. Surely this must mean that he wants me to stay? The collar and cuffs are felt with every movement, making me aware of his words and how this was his way of marking me as his.

My giddy sense of hope and belonging is countered by the arousal coursing through my body. Every step I take, every tiny movement of my hands, draws my attention to the various means of sexual torment he has bestowed upon me. I swear my breasts have swollen and tingle with each breath. My nipples are a source of fiery arousal that runs a direct line to my clit. Then there is the plug he has placed inside my ass, which makes me clench until I am throbbing with need.

How am I to get through the day?

He cleaned me up after he came inside me, which involved a great deal of intimate touching that only roused me again. I have peeled a sum of three carrots, and I already know I won't last the day, given my entire body thrums.

When Calden left, he did not say where he was going, but he will assuredly not return all day if he follows the normal pattern.

All day.

Placing the knife down with a clatter against the chopping block,

I climb down from my stool and tentatively touch my aching breasts. My nipples are hard and tingly under the strange ornate caps. I try to see if I can work out how he closed them so that I might loosen them a little.

A call goes up beyond the window, and my heart leaps into my throat. Rising onto my tiptoes, I peer out, then heave a relieved sigh when I realize it is only a group of villagers passing on their way to the river.

My heart pounds furiously as I become paranoid that he might come back and catch me touching myself, or worse, touching the caps. But no, he has gone for the day, as he usually does, leaving me here to prepare the broth! Oh, the wickedness of the centaur! He has only been gone a short time, and I cannot see how I will make it through the day. Maybe if I loosen the caps just a little now, they will not distract me so much?

I send another guilty look toward the closed door before abandoning my chores and hastening for the bedroom. The empty space beside the fur covered bed draws my eye, making me remember the strange assembly I saw in Lila's home—the saddle. Then I think about the darker, rougher version in Dires End. I nibble on my lower lip, remembering the wanton cries from Pearl as Lance rutted her.

My pussy cramps in a most alarming way before relaxing and leaving an *open* sensation.

"Oh, I don't like this at all," I mutter. I am near feverish with arousal. As I climb into the bed, I figure that I have plenty of time to make the food after I have relieved myself. His rich scent hits me the moment I lie down, and I moan softly as it shifts the plug in my ass. Turning my head to the side, I inhale the glorious scent. He said his scent acts upon me, and I can well believe it, growing a little dizzy, fingers trembling as I cup my aching breasts. The mere thought of his fingers on them, his lips sucking them until all the aches go away, only increases my fever.

I am making myself feel worse! Yet I cannot stop, and my hand skitters down, dipping into the slick folds of my pussy. Hearing a noise beyond the door, I snatch my hand away, heart racing.

Nothing. I am being foolish. He has abandoned me in this cruel state, and I have every right to do as I wish. I pull a cover across. If the beastly male returns, I will pretend I was tired. He didn't say I had to make the broth immediately, did he? Just that it must be ready for supper.

The decadently soft fur pelt acts as a source of erotic torment as it brushes over my capped nipples. I groan, unable to wait further, and satisfied that I am covered, slide my fingers down to pet my swollen pussy. Goodness, it feels so good. My attention is split between my sensitive breasts, the tail in my ass, and my fingers circling my clit. He put his cock inside me a little way, stretching me. Then earlier, when he played with the tail, working the plug in and out… Oh, it was the wickedest pleasure. I clench sharply over the plug, and my breath turns choppy. I already know I want more.

"Many centaurs do not enjoy such pleasure, but I have often thought about it. It is your own fault for having such a beautiful plump ass," he said as he pumped his fingers in and out of my ass. *"You are taking to this beautifully, my filthy, lusty little human. With some training, you might even accept the tip of my cock in here."*

My fingers move faster, making those filthy wet noises, and I am so close yet never going to get there. Now I am desperate to come. I fumble with the cap upon my breast, trying to relieve the pressure, only making it worse. I'm frustrated. I want to come so badly.

Just a little more…

The left cap pops off, releasing a great flood, just as the door opens with a great bang.

I swallow a yelp, snatching my fingers from my pussy, a flush rushing to the roots of my hair.

"Hope?" Calden calls. He is back! Goddess, why? What is he doing here?

His hooves thud as he moves around the room before coming into view.

Oh, why didn't I pull the curtain across? It might have given me a little time to compose myself.

His eyes settle on me, I am sure I am a picture of guilt, then his nostrils flare.

"I can explain," I mumble.

He smirks. "I very much doubt it."

CHAPTER TWENTY TWO

Calden

Goddess, her mischief is enough to bring a centaur to his knees. If I had any doubt that she is a highly sexual creature sent especially for me, that has fled now. I have left her all but moments, and she is in bed with her fingers busy in her pussy. The damp patch on the fur also tells a story, and my mouth waters, even as my palm itches to spank her for her naughtiness in wasting her sweet nectar.

Her eyes grow wide as saucers as I near, and she tries to make a scramble for it as I close in.

"Got you!" My reward is my arms full of a plump, wriggling woman—it is the best feeling in the world.

"Oh! Unhand me, you brute!"

"Never," I say, lifting her from the floor. Somehow, her wriggling sees my fingers slip into her drenched pussy.

She groans and goes still. "Please, Calden, I cannot bear it. I need to come."

"You have been very naughty," I say, pumping my fingers slowly, fighting not to laugh with joy. "And you came before I left. Surely you cannot need to come again?"

"I do. I really do."

"My filthy little human, you have no shame." She squeezes tight her inner muscles over my fingers in the most delightful way. "But this matter cannot be overlooked."

Reluctantly, I remove my fingers, and taking a pelt from the bed, wrap her up for decency and carry her to the table. Face pink and pretty, she nibbles on her lower lip and glances up at me.

"Hail!" A call comes from the open doorway. I got my sweet love covered just in time.

"Come in!"

She starts and peers around me as Dorn and his two apprentices enter the home. The chair is brought over and placed beside the table, while the cloth wrapped assembly is carried to the bedroom.

She heaves a breath. "Oh! What is that?"

My lips tug up as I note her flushed cheeks, the way her eyes glisten, and the unmistakable scent of her blooming arousal. "You know well what it is, Hope. I had the chair and saddling assembly commissioned the day after I found you."

Her eyes flash to meet mine. "You did?"

"Aye. It was forward of me, I know. I told myself that I must wait, that you had been through a great trauma, but I wanted you even then."

Cupping her cheek, I bring her focus to me as the sounds of hammering ensue.

"I spoke to Lila today," I say. Her pretty pink lips form a little O. "Is that why you fled? Because you thought I didn't want you?"

She nods slowly, tears pooling in her eyes. "She said you only lay with centaurs."

"That was true, Hope," I say gently, for I am still judging how she feels about this matter. "But it is not true anymore."

"But." Her eyes search mine. "We've... How? I don't know if I can?"

I stop her wild ramble with a kiss. The sounds of men hammering and called instructions continue, but my heart and arms are full of Hope and love. She opens sweetly, her tongue tangling with mine. I already feel myself rousing for her, my chest near bursting with the rich sensations she awakens in me.

"All done!" Dorn calls. I drag my lips from Hope and press my forehead to hers. She giggles prettily.

"My thanks," I call, never taking my eyes from my love. Her lips are a little puffy from my kiss, and I like that I made them so.

"I'll show myself out then!" Laughter follows as Dorn and his apprentices leave, shutting the door with a thud.

"Now," I say, brushing hair back from Hope's hot cheek. "It is time to acquaint you with the saddle. Given you are now in my moon debt indefinitely, I believe a saddling might be in order for a cherished mate."

"Mate?" she whispers, eyes cutting to the side, where the saddle is visible through the bedchamber's open curtain. I must cup her pretty flushed cheek before her eyes turn to mine.

"Aye, it's time you were saddled and accepted your place, and punishment when necessary. But I won't force this, Hope. You must want and accept this too." I search her face, needing all the words, for her to confirm that she really wants to be mine. "A centaur mates for life. I never wanted a mate before. Now, I only want you. If you can't do this, if you cannot accept me fully, then by the will of the Goddess, I will set you free."

"Free?! Oh, no, I very much want my punishment. I deserve my punishment!"

"The saddle is not only for punishment," I say, feeling my cock thrust fully from the sheath at her enthusiasm, heavy, long, and dripping near constantly upon the floor. "It is for mounting and mating too. We are long overdue taking the final step. Mayhap today is the day you shall fully belong to me."

"Today?" she squeaks out. "You mean today…that you will claim me today?"

"Assuredly, I will. I did not bring it home before, for I did not trust myself not to saddle and mount you before you were ready. If you accept me, if you accept this, then I do not want to wait anymore. I will go as slowly as I must, my sweet woman, but we both need this. The memory of you in that terrible place, the image of you in that filthy farm under the influence of a witch, needs to be purged for both our sakes. The saddle and station are the safest place, especially for the first time."

"Please," she says, pretty brown eyes meeting mine. "I want to, although I admit that I am nervous, but I trust you. I have trusted you with my life, how could I not trust you similarly with this?"

There is no more time for words or second-guessing. She has said she wants this, as do I. Removing the pelt, I carry her to the bedroom. Here I stop, nostrils flared, assaulted by strong emotions as I see the saddle there in my room. "This is yours, Hope—a saddle I have ordered made especially, and only, for you."

"It is beautiful," she murmurs, drawing my eyes to her.

"It is, my love, and it will be so much more beautiful once you are upon it." I sit her on the saddle, loving how it places her perfectly for me, my gaze lowering to her pretty plump tits. They are swollen. The left one, where she removed the cap, leaks the sweet stickiness I have come to crave. When I cup it and gently squeeze, a little bit of clear liquid trickles out. I swallow, feeling the weight of them in my hands. "My poor sweet lass, no wonder you are in distress."

She nods, her face glowing, biting her lip. "Please, Calden."

I squeeze, riveted by the clear liquid beading at her nipple. "There, I am charged with your care now. It is my duty to ensure

L.V. LANE

you are comfortable, and the Goddess would assuredly not wish this bounty to be wasted."

I lap the stiff peak with my tongue before closing my lips over the plump mound and sucking. We both groan, her from relief, me from pure masculine joy as I suckle her warm goodness into my belly.

Hope

My hips rock slowly as I grow needy again. Goddess, his words drive me near as insensible as his clever fingers and tongue do. The air is filled with his scent, and I know without looking his cock will have fully pushed from the sheath and is likely leaking pre-cum in a long thread to the floor.

"Please!" I say, desperate for him to tend to the other side. "Oh, please remove the cap. I cannot stand it anymore."

It is not only about the cap, for everything is spinning, and I must clench my fingers in his hair, lest I fall.

He gifts me with such a wicked smirk that I quake with heated anticipation. He will not be rushed. There is punishment still to be had. How I want everything he will give me, how thrilled I am that he had a saddle made especially and only for me.

"This is perfectly natural," he says, thumb brushing over the cap, making me squirm anew as it sets off a tightening low in my womb. "You will need to be rutted often once I claim you, will demand it, or so I have heard."

I shudder as he plays with the cap, teasing me to distraction. I already know I will want him often. I want him now, and I have not even taken him yet. My feelings transcend my body's limitations, existing in a different, otherworldly sphere. "Please, Calden."

His eyes gleam darkly as he presses kisses against the plump flesh near the cap, which twists as he flicks it with his fingers. My legs part further. All shame is gone as I rock against the saddle, drenched with need.

Popping off the cap, he closes his mouth over the distended peak in a shocking move that sends a shot of pleasure straight to my aching pussy. I squeal, jiggling about. He toys with my other nipple as he sucks me, making all the sensations twist up together. I fist his hair, holding him to me, while the sweet rhythmic pull of his mouth, as he tends to one side and then the other, leaves me gasping.

"Oh, I'm going to… I'm coming." My pussy spasms sharply and falls into contractions as he drains me. Were his strong arm not clasped around me, I would surely collapse, for I turn limp with pleasure.

His lips pop off, and he pins me with a look. "Lie back, love. I will secure you while I open your pretty cunt all up."

I swallow, a little nervous and a lot aroused by his bold words.

"I'm going to bind you," he announces. "It is important that you do not move while I am doing this, lest you hurt yourself. After you have softened for me, I will turn you over."

I nod. He gathers my hands, kissing them reverently before securing my cuffs above my head. He moves around, hooves thudding softly against the floor. My legs are parted, knees bent, and my ankles tied to the saddle, leaving me open and exposed to his lustful gaze. He pauses to fondle my breasts. "Beautiful. I love these pretty tits." His hand skitters down my belly until he settles over my pussy. "Drenched," he murmurs, sliding his fingers over my swollen pussy. "Even your cunt is plump and pretty, designed to hold a cock as it thrusts in and out."

"Oh please!"

"You will wait," he says, face implacable as he pets me.

I try to lift my hips, groaning when I find I am thoroughly trapped. Ugh, why did I agree to this? Calden has addled my mind as he circles my clit with his thumb and thrusts his fingers shallowly in and out. I chant under my breath, begging for more and to be filled All the nerves flutter and awaken, my breathing shifting as the pleasure grows.

"I think some reins might be in order," he says.

I clench around his fingers.

His chuckle is low and steeped with masculine satisfaction. "Ah, my love. You like the sound of that, do you?"

"Yes. Please let me come."

"No." He torments me, giving me pleasure but never quite enough, working fingers in, face determined.

Then his fingers disappear completely, and he licks the length of my pussy.

"Umnnn!"

He eats me like he is ravenous and cannot get enough, lips moving over me, tongue delving deeply into my core before he laps at my clit again. I'm rising, and there is no stopping it now as I reach ever higher, while as he brands himself upon me, until finally, I come, gasping, clenching, opening.

His head lifts, and he thrusts three thick fingers into my pussy, finding that sensitive spot on the inner front wall and petting it without mercy.

I groan, twitch, and try to get away.

"Again," he rumbles. "Come again for me, now."

It is too much, too intense, but I cannot escape, and my whole body twists up, sweat breaking out across my skin as I come for him, this one even stronger.

I feel him reach, going deeper still, fingers rotating in me, his knuckles... Goddess, what is he doing?

"You are dilating nicely," he says, thrusting deeper, making me pant. The sounds, as he fingers me, are wet and sticky. "You need to take much more before you can fully accept my beastly cock. Now, open up like a good girl."

"Oh!"

I come again. It washes over me, making me achy and ever needier. I cannot look, but my imagination runs rampant, and I know he is deep inside me. I can feel his knuckles as he breeches my entrance with them.

"Deep breath."

I shake my head.

"Take a nice deep breath for me, Hope. Right now."

His stern voice compels me, and I do, sucking air into my starved lungs. I feel him slip all the way in, settling inside me so deeply, his hand curling in, forming a fist.

His thumb brushes back and forth lightly over my clit.

"Beautiful."

I blink tears from my eyes, trying to find ground. Everything is centered upon the intense fullness of Calden being inside me, filling me.

"Oh Goddess!"

"Come, love. Come all over me, open for me, and I will claim you fully. I will bridle and rein and mount you, and make you mine."

His knuckles moves the tiniest amount inside me, and I spin into the wildest, most incredible climax of my life. I squeal, gulping for breath.

The straps are loosened, and he kisses me lovingly, but as he lifts his head and meets my eyes, I see the heat. His lust is dark and intense, and I want all of it.

"It's time, Hope," he says, carefully lifting and turning me face down in the saddle. As he binds me in this new position, the air thickens with the scent of lust. His pheromones are rich and potent, and I am ravenous for more of him.

He is going to mount me. I experience no fear, only deep arousal. My pussy feels open, dilating, he said. It aches to be filled.

He pinches the nearest nipple, squeezing it, coaxing it to full hardness before applying a weighted clamp.

"Oh! What?" I squirm with frustration when the bindings hold me tight.

"Breathe through it," he says, tone brooking no arguments, and rounding me, he performs the same torment to the other side.

I do, gulping breath, hearing an unmistakable splat as my pussy weeps.

"There, does that feel good?"

I mutter nonsense as he tugs them lightly, ensuring I am thoroughly stimulated before reins are attached to my collar and clamped nipples. He shakes the reins, and I squeal as heat passes from my nipples to my core. "Ah, so good. Please, I cannot wait anymore. Don't make me wait."

"Indeed, you are ready, sweet love," he announces. "My beautiful Hope, all saddled and bridled. I must claim you now, for I, too, can no longer wait."

My emotional state is one of deep love and gratitude. My body thrums with arousal all the greater because I cherish him so. There is no more waiting. He rises up, hooves skittering and clattering into the slots, sending a thrill coursing through me.

I feel the brush of his fur covered belly against my ass, followed by the slick passage of his probing cock.

He groans, low and long as the tip snags the slippery entrance to my pussy. I fidget, wanting more of the enticing fullness, moaning when I remember that I am thoroughly trapped.

"Steady, love." His hooves clatter as he sinks deeper, sliding his hot thick cock into me slowly.

I whimper.

"I have got you, Hope. Relax and let your hot little cunt open for me."

I have no choice. Calden keeps sinking, and I groan as my pussy is forced to yield to his hot length, filling me to capacity. I feel like I can't breathe, like he is inside my belly.

He stills, heavy cock throbbing and flexing inside me, and I am throbbing around him.

Then he jangles the reins, and pleasure blooms. My pussy clenching fiercely over his fat cock is terrifying and arousing beyond all understanding. A deep guttural cry is torn from my lips. "Goddess, I'm going to come."

"Come if you need to, love," he says.

He begins to rut me with deep, heavy strokes that speak of his immense power, filling me all up over and over. I keep coming, convulsing in waves of pleasure that never seem to end.

"Let me all the way in," he rumbles.

In? Is he not already in?

I hang over the saddle, lost in a haze of madness as he ruts me ever deeper. There is so much of him, too much, yet he somehow fits. My pussy gushes, sending splatters over my thighs and the floor with every thrust. The monstrous thudding as he slams in and out makes the assembly creak and groan. He is so powerful as he towers over me, a great beastly male with unearthly lust.

And I want it all, pussy squeezing over him like I don't want to let him out. No sensitive inner nerve escapes the surge and retreat of his cock, sending me reeling into euphoria.

"Please, I need more." I know not this mumbled nonsense that pops from my lips.

His low chuckle is pure male pride, and he takes me harder, pounding me into the saddle, slaking his lust with every deep drive. "Your hot cunt was made to take a centaur's cock. You will be well ruined for all others when I am done. My lusty mate, begging for me. Do you want me to breed you, love?"

"Goddess, please, yes!" Just the thought of him filling me with seed, breeding a child in me, sets me spinning and clenching so hard over his rutting length that I see stars.

He roars, slams deep, and stills. I throb around him, and deep inside, I feel the first hot splash of his cum. A climax rolls through me, setting me convulsing around him in deep contractions that never seem to end, coaxing more and more of his seed until my pussy and belly ache, and still, he comes.

"Good girl," he croons. "Let me fill you all up."

He rocks gently, flexing his length inside me. I whimper, sure I cannot take anymore, but I do, and another climax sweeps through me.

He groans, rocking as I clamp down over him. "My balls ache with the strain of trying to fill your hungry cunt." He slips from me in a rush, hooves clattering and thudding as they hit the ground.

I shudder, my pussy falling into more contractions, pushing out a great flood of cum. "Oh!"

"Steady." His voice calms me as his fingers gently probe. Through the curtain of my hair, I can see his thick, long cock jerk with interest, and I groan.

"Goddess, that is an arresting sight. You are gaping, love."

I can feel how open I am. "Oh please, I don't like it. Please fill me again."

He plays with me, making wet sticky noises. My pussy cramps viciously, and another great flood splatters onto the floor.

"There is no room in your tiny body, sweet mate. Let me help you." He pumps his fingers into my pussy vigorously. The cramping starts again as more and more cum splatters and trickles down my thighs until I am an empty, shaky mess.

The scent of his seed makes me dizzy. My nipples ache, but my pussy aches more.

"I've rutted you hard, my love, and I thought it would be enough, but it is not. I'm going to need to rut you again, harder still. You are mine now, my mate. Mine to rut, whenever and however I may choose."

He does not lie, doing all that he promises and more, and I love every moment of it.

I wake up in the bed, wrapped up in his arms, warm and the best kind of achy.

"How are you feeling, love?"

As I blink up at him through the early dawn light, a smile blooms upon my face. "A little sore," I admit shyly. "Are we mated now?"

"Before the Goddess, we are mated," he says. "Did I not rut you well enough? Did I not show you my love?"

Love. Such a simple word, yet it holds a myriad of meanings. I loved my mother and father. I thought I loved Karl briefly, although now I understand that I did not. The feelings I have for Calden are a thousand times more nuanced than anything I have felt before.

"I think so," I say, biting my lip to hide my smile. "My breasts are a little swollen. I think they might need tending to. I believe it is a mate's duty to see to such things."

"Insatiable," he says, but he is already hoisting me up the bed and latching onto the nearest nipple. I am in bliss.

He takes his time and is gentle, and the sensation is oh so sweet. Before long, I grow restless with need, riding his thick fingers as he pets the sensitive slick gland, as he calls it, with the same agonizing gentleness until I come in a sweet climax.

"You are plump and pretty everywhere," he says, nuzzling the side of my breast as he slows his fingers. "Even drained, your tits are still more than my big hands can hold. Your hips and ass are similarly generous. There is not an inch of your perfect body that wasn't sent by the Goddess to entice a male to rut."

The truth of his words is evidenced in his open, loving expression. This is how he really sees me. I can only wonder that he thinks I am so perfect, when I similarly find him as perfect in my eyes.

"I love you," I say. "I love you so much, and I'm so sorry that I ran."

He pulls me close against him, wrapping me up in his arms and his love. "And I you, sweet Hope. Until the Goddess claims one of us to her side, I am yours, and you shall be mine."

My tummy suddenly rumbles. I'm trying not to look, but too late, I see that his cock has pushed from the sheath, and a long thread of pre-cum leaks all the way to the pelt.

He chuckles.

I blush furiously.

"Go ahead, love," he says. "Given you are well bred after our mating, little wonder you are hungry."

My eyes widen as I take in what he says. With child? Joy crashes through me, only spoiled when my tummy rumbles loudly again.

I cannot wait. I need him.

"Steady, love," he says, chuckling as I all but fall over his legs in my eagerness to get to my treat.

I tend him with the same loving reverence he did me. My mind wants to wallow in imagining the joyful future ahead of us, but I tamp it down, for I wish to be in this moment and savor it. So I love and worship him with my mouth until he gifts me his seed, and then, when I come down from the powerful climax, I nestle in his arms, content and safe.

EPILOGUE

Calden

"I'm not sure this is a good idea," Hope says as I pick her up and place her over my back.

"This is an excellent idea," I say. "You have a former home with personal things, which are a legacy from your late mother. It is only right that you should have them back. Mayhap the spineless bastard has already moved on, but if he hasn't, it will be my pleasure to deal with him."

She frets until I stamp my hooves, forcing her to focus on holding onto me, although I'm watching her every move and there's not a chance I would let my love fall. With a squeak, she throws her arms around my waist.

I chuckle.

"That was wicked," she says. "I might have fallen off!"

"Never," I say. "You know me better than that. Now hold tight, and we shall be there before lunchtime, even at a steady pace."

We set off through the forest, waving to the two sentries on the lake's edge. It's a pleasant morning, and I admit I enjoy the feel of her against my back. She has changed since she first arrived here as a sweet, broken lass escaping raiders and wearing the hideous, heavy clothes humans favor. Now look at her. She has bloomed under my care, and I feel a fierce surge of pride that this sweet lass has come to love me, a centaur, who is half beast. To be accepted willingly, gladly, and joyfully, and to receive and give the pleasure we share, is to understand contentment at the highest level. My love for her swells, encompassing the child she now carries.

I will see the heirlooms left by her mother are passed on to our children, where it is within my power to do so. There are other things in her former home that she might want, memories through keepsakes. With this in mind, a pack horse follows, so we can bring back more if needed.

Excepting any clothes, for she will assuredly not be wearing human clothes again.

Our pace is a slow walk through the forest, my spear in hand lest we encounter trouble, while I enjoy her body against mine. Her scent fills my lungs, her lush breasts press against my back, and her hot cunt makes my coat damp where her thighs are spread open around me.

"We might need a small break," I say, glancing back. It amazes me that she can still blush after all the ways I've enjoyed her sweet body. "My cock is hard. I will never reach Melwood without some relief."

She giggles, her hands tightening around my waist. "I'm a little hungry," she confesses.

"Well, it's hardly surprising, given you are with child. Here, this is a nice spot. We shall rest in the shade of this tree." I draw to a stop and help her down, eager to feed my mate. My cock is already long and hard, and my balls are heavy. The mere thought that she might be hungry drives my own need to provide for her.

The moment I settle against the loamy forest floor, she crawls over me on her hands and knees, eager for her treat. I part my stifles, giving her full access so she might feed. She does, and I swear I am the luckiest centaur as I watch a pretty flush fill her cheeks. She licks and laps the tip of my cock, knowing how to grip and stroke to drive her mate to the heights of pleasure, encouraging me to spill.

"I am close, love," I say.

One small hand lowers to cup my balls, rolling them gently, coaxing me to come.

I do, shooting into her willing mouth, my legs twitching as the pleasure surges through me. Eyes hooded, I gather up her hair, groaning as rapture plays out on her face. She licks and sucks me dry, then plays with my balls, encouraging the last and deepest gush.

"There, love, I have not a drop left."

She is stuffing her fingers in her mouth and humming contentedly as I gather her in my arms, and my eyes lower to her tits. They are full and often sore. She's blessed twice, and I, the lucky recipient. "Are you sore, love?" I ask. "Would you like me to tend to you?"

"Please," she says, her fingers turning clumsy as they tug open the fastening that holds her lush tits. The moment one escapes the cursed confines she insists upon, my lips close over the tip. She sobs with pleasure as I suckle the sweet goodness all up. "Oh please, I need…" I squeeze her tit roughly as I feast upon it, which is how she sometimes needs. "Yes, that feels so good." She thrusts her tit against my face, encouraging me to be rougher still. There was a time when I thought myself too brutish for such a sweet mate, but now I see we are perfect.

I drain her left tit, then start on the right, just as my seed works on her belly, driving her to climax. My fingers slip between her parted thighs, and I thrust three thick fingers into her hot cunt as she turns rigid, pussy spasming as my seed goes to work. I watch the rapture contort her face as I drain her right tit. As she gasps and groans her pleasure, her pussy clamps over my thrusting fingers.

We share a lusty kiss as my fingers turn gentle. "Look here," I say. "You have made a little mess, sweet lass. Best I clean you all up."

"Goddess," she says. "I'm too sensitive."

My grin is wicked as I pull her around to my liking, bury my head between her thighs, and feast once again. She comes twice more and has another feed before she is fully satisfied. By the time we are done, she is limp and well sated, and the sun is high in the sky. We cuddle for a little while before we must be on our way.

Hope

When Calden announces it's time to carry on, my nerves return. It feels like forever since I was last in Melwood, where I was born and spent all my life until the fateful day when I met Calden.

I know I need closure, but what will I find? Mayhap Karl and Fiona are already gone. Perhaps they found my mother's jewels, and how ridiculous I left them hidden away and never showed them to him. Well, not me. My mother always left them in a safe place, save for a few occasions when they were worn. I doubt Karl would ever think to look under the old oak table, where there is a secret compartment. Still, I can't readily anticipate what I should find on arrival, nor how I shall feel. I am mated now and have a new life. Calden is a revelation, but perhaps the villagers will think strangely of me for mating with a centaur. Their opinions will not sway me. My mate is noble and proud. He is kind, and he cares for me and keeps me safe. He is generous in his loving and in giving of pleasure.

I carry his child.

There could be no better man, beast, or creature of any kind that I would give my heart to. I cannot wait to meet the new life growing within me. All centaurs born of mixed race start as a human baby. Only later do they change. Some shift once and stay a centaur for

THE CENTAUR IN MY VALLEY

the rest of their life, and others can shift back and forth at will. I
hope there shall be more little girls and boys who will reflect both of
us. With Calden's steady influence, I know our children will thrive
within the herd, where the Goddess' ways are strong.

My heart rate quickens as we crest the rise in the forest path and
the first rooftops of Melwood come into view. Melwood is a sleepy
little town nestled in the foothills of the valley. Beyond is a smaller
village of Andell, to the north is a castle, to the east is the sea, and to
the west are the mountains where the shifters live.

Centaurs are a mysterious and private race, and I wonder what
the people of Melwood will think upon seeing one, and me with
one...and my new attire, which is nothing like the sensible, heavy
dresses I used to wear.

As we draw ever nearer, villagers stop and stare, calling to one
another, gathering on doorsteps, and come out to see what this is
about, calling out greetings as they recognize me.

"Hope is here! She has returned! Praise the Goddess!"

I see familiar faces I have lived among all my life.

"Hope!" Mary cries, wiping hands on her apron and hurrying
down the little cobbled path of her cottage to meet me at the path.
"Goddess be blessed! You are safe!"

Calden stops and helps me down so that I might go and hug my
dear friend. "What a sight! We thought for sure you had gone,
snatched by raiders. A party went in search after Karl came back.
The lord himself gathered men and horses, but you were long gone,
and the onset of night forced them to come back. It was the worst
of days. Oh, how we wept. But here you are and looking so hail.
How did you get away?" She looks between Calden and me and then
back to me again.

A small crowd has gathered around us, eyeing Calden warily.
"Calden happened upon us and rescued me." I turn, lifting my hand
to Calden, who takes it within his, smiling and reminding me that he

is here and with him, I am always safe. "We are mated now."

Mary laughs and hugs me again. "How wonderful to see you, how you glow. Look at what you wear!"

I blush, stirring a chuckle from Calden, for he knows I am still very much shy about showing so much skin in a hide dress that barely skims my knees. Certainly, it is not a dress that a village woman would wear.

"Are you returning to your cottage?" one woman calls out. "How we missed you."

"And her skills with a needle," one man calls good-naturedly to the laughter of the crowd. "My wife swears you are the best seamstress in the land. Costs me twice the penny to send her things to the city."

"You can afford it, ya miser!" another man ribs.

"I came back to collect my mother's things from the cottage," I say. "Is it...is it still there?

"Aye," Mary says, lips thinning. "It is. Karl lives there with Fiona, although nobody speaks to them. Lord Melwood was not impressed he left you as he did, and Fiona... Well, not many liked her afore she set up in your home barely the next day after you were lost. Still, it is your home, passed to you by your mother and father."

I turn toward Calden, finding censure and anger glittering on his face in anticipation of dealing with my former husband.

"What will you do?" Mary asks. The once jovial crowd is now quiet, waiting.

"She will take back what is rightfully hers," Calden says, speaking for the first time. A proud, noble creature, he is otherworldly in his magnificence here, among this simple village.

"As is your right," a man calls. Others murmur their agreement.

"And if her former husband, that weak male, is still there when we arrive, I'll be sure to toss him out."

Mary's eyes turn round before her face splits in a grin.

The crowd murmurs turn to ones of approval as Calden lifts me to his back. "Show me the way, Hope."

The villagers call to one another, gathering more and more, and they follow in our wake as we make our way down the lane. They call out greetings, and I wave back, heartened to see so many people who are friends and acquaintances, feeling my heart lifted by their evident joy in seeing me well.

As my little cottage comes into view, my hands tighten around Calden.

"Is this your home, love?" he asks, glancing back at me.

"It is," I say, just as the door creaks open and a bedraggled Karl stumbles out.

"Down you get, lass," Calden says, voice deepening as his warrior side comes to the fore. "Better not be too close, lest you come to harm."

Karl's jaw hangs slack as he looks between me, Calden, and the gathered crowd. He takes a stumbled step back. "Hope?"

"Karl? What's going on?" a feminine voice calls from the cottage. The last time I heard that voice, she was encouraging my husband to poison me so that she might live in comfort in my house.

My lips tremble a little. Mary comes to my side, placing her arm around me.

The door slams open again, and Fiona storms out.

"Is this them?" Calden asks, turning to me. "Is this the man who abandoned you to raiders? Is this his lover who wished to put poison in your tea and steal your mother's heirlooms?"

I hear collective gasps from the surrounding crowd.

"I never poisoned her," Fiona says, squaring her shoulders to make herself look tough. "It was just nonsense talk between lovers. The lass lies."

Calden takes a single step forward, and both Karl and Fiona cower back. "No man nor woman shall call my mate a liar. You have moments to leave. Take nothing that is not yours and get out of this village. Do not dare to ever come back. We centaurs have our own ways of dealing with those who wronged us, and it is not civilized." He hefts his spear, planting the butt against the dusty path.

Around us, the crowd is silent.

"I'm not leaving," Fiona says, face contorting with her fury. "She is a liar. She has bedded a centaur."

I hold my breath as Calden's knuckles tighten on the spear.

"Peace," a booming voice calls, and we all turn as Lord Melwood steps forward. "Hope, tell me, without fear, are these accusations true?"

"Yes, milord," I say. "They are. I came home early from an errand in the village. That's when I overheard them together, talking in my bedroom. Karl came after me, said he would leave with Fiona and not take my things. That's when the raiders came. They rode throughout the day and camped for the night... They were about to... That's when Calden came. I wish no harm toward them, but I want to collect my mother's things, if they are still there."

"Get your things," Karl says, thrusting Fiona back toward the home.

"But— "

"For fuck's sake. Get your things." He follows her into the house, and they return shortly with two small bags.

"I don't have all my things," Fiona wails.

"Leave them," Karl replies.

As they go to scurry past, Calden moves to block their path.

"Go and check if your things are there, Hope. They are going nowhere until you are satisfied that you have what is yours."

I head into the house, and how strange it is to be inside here. Everything is so familiar, and yet it is no longer my home. I find everything where it should be, and seeing those few jewels rekindles memories of my mother wearing them. I doubt they have real value, save for sentimentality. Karl would have been disappointed should he have tried to sell them. Still, they are mine, and I shall pass them on to my children one day.

I return outside. "They are here," I call.

Calden steps aside. "Be gone," he says. "And do not think to return."

They leave on foot—a pitiful sight that makes me sad it has come to this.

"Well, then," says Lord Melwood. "I am glad to find you hail and well, Hope. Does this mean you might return?" He turns to his wife, who stands at his side. "My dear wife misses your beautiful sewing and your chats over tea."

"No, my lord, I am not, for I am now mated to Calden and carry his child."

"How wonderful," says Lady Melwood, coming to join me. She takes my hand. "It is like a fairy tale, a chosen one going to live among the centaurs. And what a fine mate you have!"

"Aye, milady," I say. "I have." I share a look with Calden, seeing his pride and how it is equal to mine for him. "I will gather a few things that are personal to me. And then I hope that the home might be gifted to a young couple or family who are in need of the space."

"Worry not, lass," Lord Melwood says. "We shall find good keepers for your former home."

I spend the rest of the day in the village, chatting to friends and reminiscing. Then, as afternoon turns toward evening, we must be on our way.

I say goodbye to the villagers and my former home.

I have a new home now, and a mate I feel blessed with.

"Are you ready, Hope?" he asks.

"I am, milord."

He chuckles at my mischief. "Just Calden, lass."

"I am ready, Calden."

So, with my late mother's heirlooms and a heart full of hope, we set off on the journey home, to the waves and well-wishes of the villagers.

The End.

ABOUT THE AUTHOR

I love a happily ever after, although sometimes the journey to get there can be rough on my poor characters.

An unashamed fan of the alpha, the antihero, and the throwback in all his guises and wherever he may lurk.

I'm a new author, learning as I go and appreciate feedback of all kinds.

Drop me a message and let me know what you think.

Website: www.authorlvlane.com
Facebook Page: www.facebook.com/LVLaneAuthor/
Facebook group: www.facebook.com/groups/LVLane/
Goodreads: www.goodreads.com/LVLane

Made in United States
Orlando, FL
27 April 2022

17274856R00121